FALCON BOOKS

Jean Craig Finds Romance

BY KAY LYTTLETON

Jean Craig had always wanted to be an artist. But when her family had moved to Woodhow in Connecticut, she had given up her art lessons. Later, when she was able to resume them, she realized how important a career was to her. But then Ralph McRae came along, and Jean found herself unable to make up her mind as to what she wanted most. And while Jean was trying to come to a decision, her sister Kit was having a fine adventure of her own out West.

Jean Craig Finds Romance is filled with gaiety and humor, another charming story of the wonderful, courageous Craigs and their family adventures.

Other FALCON BOOKS for Girls:

JEAN CRAIG GROWS UP
JEAN CRAIG IN NEW YORK
JEAN CRAIG, NURSE
PATTY AND JO, DETECTIVES
CHAMPION'S CHOICE

A startling procession came from the river.

JEAN CRAIG
FINDS ROMANCE

by KAY LYTTLETON

THE WORLD PUBLISHING COMPANY

CLEVELAND AND NEW YORK

Falcon Books

are published by THE WORLD PUBLISHING COMPANY

2231 West 110th Street · Cleveland 2 · Ohio

Contents

1. Kit Traps a Thief   9

2. I Smell Smoke   21

3. The Important Letter   29

4. Kit's Plan   36

5. Farewell Party   47

6. "The Boy's" Arrival   55

7. The House Under the Bluff   70

8. A Square Deal   86

9. Hope College   98

10. The Suprise   109

11. The Mysterious Guest 121

12. Homesick 131

13. Frank Apologizes 138

14. The Secret in the Urn 150

15. Home Again 168

16. Visiting Celebrities 177

17. Frank to the Rescue 195

18. Jean's Romance 206

JEAN CRAIG FINDS ROMANCE

1. Kit Traps a Thief

Kit was on lookout duty, and had been for the past hour and a half. The windows of one of the upstairs bedrooms commanded a view of a large part of the countryside, and from here she had done sentry duty over the huckleberry patch.

It lay to the northeast of the house, a great, rambling, rocky, ten-acre lot that straggled unevenly from the wood road down to the river. To the casual onlooker, it seemed just a patch of underbrush. There were half-grown-birches all over it, and now and then a little dwarf spruce tree or cluster of hazel bushes. But to the Craig family that ten-acre lot represented

profit in the month of August when huckleberries and blueberries were ripe.

The Craig family were newcomers to the
country, newcomers in the eyes of the natives
of Elmhurst, Connecticut, for they had moved
there a year and a half ago seeking peace and
rest for Mr. Craig, who was slowly recovering
from a nervous breakdown. The family's adventures and problems in making their home
in the country were told in *Jean Craig Grows Up*.
Jean, eighteen and ambitious for an artist's
career, had spent part of the previous winter
studying in a New York art school and her ex-
periences there were described in *Jean Craig in
New York*.

Sixteen-year-old Kit, in whom the spirit of
adventure ran high, was watching suspiciously
a trim-looking, red-wheeled, black-bodied truck,
driven by a strange man, as it pulled up at the
pasture bars and stopped. The man took out
of the truck not a burlap bag, but a tan leather
case and also something else that looked like a
large box with a handle on it.

"Camouflage," said Kit to herself, scornfully. "He's going to fill them with our berries, and then make believe he's selling books."

Downstairs she tore with the news. Her twelve-year-old brother Tommy and his pal Jack Davis, nine, were out in the barn negotiating peace terms with a half-grown calf that they had been trying to tame for days, and which still persisted in butting its head every time they came near it with friendly overtures. Jack, whose mother had died and whose father had not wanted to be bothered with him, had come to live with the Craigs after Jean and Tommy had discovered him in Nantic a few days before Christmas, lost and alone. Tommy had immediately assumed responsibility for Jack and protected and bossed him as if Jack were his special property.

Jean and Doris, who was fourteen, had gone up to Norwich with Mrs. Craig for the day, and Mr. Craig was out in the apple orchard with Philip Weaver, spraying the trees against the attacks of the gypsy moths. At least,

Philip held to spraying, but Mr. Craig was anxious to experiment with some of the newer methods advocated by the government.

Kit called her news to Tommy and he and Jack started off after the trespasser, while she went back to telephone Mr. Hicks, the constable. The very last thing she had said to Tommy was to put the vandal in the corncrib and stand guard over him until Mr. Hicks came.

"Don't you worry one bit, Miss Kit," the Constable of Elmhurst Township assured her over the phone. "I'll be there in my car in less than twenty minutes. You folks ain't the only ones that's suffering this year from fruit thieves, and it's time we taught these high fliers from town that they can't light anywhere they like and pick what they like. I'll take him right down to the judge this afternoon."

Kit sat by the open window and fanned herself with a feeling of triumphant indignation. If Jean or Doris had been home, she knew perfectly well they would have been soft-hearted and lenient, but every berry on every bush was precious to Kit, and she felt that now was the appointed hour to catch the thief.

Inside of a few minutes Tommy and Jack came back hot and red-faced, but filled with the pride of accomplishment.

"We've got him," Tommy said, happily, "safe and sound in the corncrib, and it's hotter than all get out in there. He can't escape unless he slips through a crack in the floor. We just caught him as he was bending down right over the bushes, and what do you suppose he tried to tell us, Kit? He said he was looking for caterpillars." Tommy laughed. "Did you call up Mr. Hicks?"

Kit nodded, looking out at the corncrib. The midsummer sun beat down upon it pitilessly, at the end of the lane behind the bar.

"Gosh, do you suppose he'll survive, Tommy? I'll bet it's a hundred and six inside there."

"Aw, it'll do him good," put in Jack. "Don't you worry about him. He's a strong man. It was all Tommy and I could do to keep a good hold on him."

"Oh, kids," exclaimed Kit. "I didn't want you to touch him."

"How else were we to catch him?" demanded Tommy. "You and your bright ideas. Come on, Jack, let's go back and stand guard over him."

Kit watched them leave rather dubiously. It was one thing to act on the impulse of the moment and quite another to face the consequences. Now that the prisoner was safe in the corncrib, she wondered uneasily just what her father would say when he found out what she had done to protect the berry patch. But just now he was in the upper orchard with old Mr. Weaver, deep in apple culture, and she thought she could get rid of the trespasser before he returned.

Mrs. Gorham was in the kitchen putting up peaches. She was humming and the sound came through the screen door. Mrs. Gorham was Judge Ellis' housekeeper and helped out the Craigs occasionally when an extra hand was needed. Now that Judge Ellis had married Becky Craig, Mr. Craig's cousin who had engineered the family's move to Woodhow and was always at hand in an emergency, Mrs. Gorham was not needed as much at the Judge's home. Billie, the Judge's grandson who was sixteen and Doris's best friend, completed the Ellis household.

Kit slipped around the drive behind the house out to the hill road. Mr. Hicks would have to come from this direction, and here she sat on the ground at the entrance to the driveway, thinking and waiting.

The minutes passed and still Mr. Hicks failed to appear. If Kit could have visualized his trip, she might have imagined him lingering here and there along the country roads, stopping to tell the news to any neighbor who might be nearby. Beside him sat Elvira, his youngest, drinking in every word with tense appreciation of the novelty. It was the first chance Mr. Hicks had had to make an arrest during his term of office, and as a special test and reward of diligence, Elvira had been permitted to come along and behold the climax with her own eyes. But the twenty minutes stretched out into nearly forty, and Kit's heart sank when she saw her father strolling leisurely down the orchard path, just as Mr. Hicks hove in sight.

Mr. Weaver limped beside him, smiling contentedly.

"Well, I guess we've got 'em licked this time, Tom," he chuckled. "If there's a bug or a moth that can stand that dose of mine, I'll eat the whole apple crop myself."

"Still, I'll feel better satisfied when Howard gets here, and gives an expert opinion," Mr. Craig replied. "He wrote he expected to be here today without fail."

"Well, of course you're entitled to your opinion, Tom," Mr. Weaver replied, doubtfully. "But I never did set any store at all by these here government boys with their little satchels and tree doctor books. I'd just as soon walk up to an apple tree and hand it a blue pill or a shin plaster."

Kit stood up hastily as Mr. Hicks drove in from the road.

"Hello," he called out, "How are you, Tom? Howdy, Philip? Miss Kit here tells me you've been harboring a fruit thief, and you've caught him."

Kit's cheeks were bright red as she laid one hand on her father's shoulder.

"Tommy's got him right over in the corn-crib, Mr. Hicks. I haven't told Dad yet, because it might worry him. It isn't anything at all, Dad," she added, hurriedly. "We have been keeping a watch on the berry patch, and today it was my turn. I just happened to see somebody over there after the berries, so I told Tommy and Jack to go and get him, and I called up Mr. Hicks."

Mr. Craig shook his head with a little smile. "I'm afraid Kit has been overambitious, Mr.

Hicks," he said. "I don't know anything about this, but we'll go over to the corncrib and find out what it's all about."

Kit and Evie secured a good vantage point up on the porch while the others skirted around the garden over to the old corncrib where Tommy and Jack stood guard.

"My, I like your place over here," Evie exclaimed, wistfully. "You've got so many flowers. Mom says she can't even grow a nasturtium on our place without the hens scratching it up."

Kit nodded, but could not answer. Already she felt that all was not as it should be at the corncrib. She saw Tommy stealthily and cautiously put back the wide wooden bars that held the door, then Mr. Hicks, fully on the defensive with a stout hickory cane held in readiness for any unseemly move on the part of the culprit, advanced into the corncrib. Evie drew closer, her little freckled face full of curiosity.

"Isn't Pop brave?" she whispered, "and he

never made but two arrests before in all his life. One was over at Miss Hornaby's when she wouldn't let Minnie and Myron go to school 'cause their shoes were all out on the ground, and the other time he got that weaver over at Beacon Hill for selling cider."

Still Kit had no answer, for over at the corn-crib she saw the strangest scene. Out stepped the prisoner as fearlessly and blithely as possible, spoke to her father, and the two of them instantly shook hands, while Tommy, Jack, Mr. Hicks, and Mr. Weaver stared with all their might. The next the girls knew, the whole party came strolling back leisurely, and Kit could see the stranger was regaling her father with a humorous view of the whole affair. Tommy tried to signal to her behind his back some mysterious warning, and even Mr. Hicks looked jocular.

Kit leaned both hands on the railing, and stared hard at the trespasser. He was a young man, dressed in a light gray suit with high laced boots to protect him from briars. He was fair-skinned, but tanned so deeply that his blond, curly hair seemed even lighter. He smiled at Kit, with one foot on the lower step, while Mr. Craig called up, "Kit, my dear, this is Mr. Howard, our fruit expert from Washington, whom I was expecting."

And Kit nodded, blushing furiously and wishing with all her heart she might have silenced Evie's audible and disappointed remark, "Didn't he hook huckleberries after all?"

2. I Smell Smoke

"I was perfectly positive that if we went away and left you in charge for one single day, Kit, you would manage to get into some kind of trouble," Jean said reproachfully that evening. "If you only wouldn't act on the impulse of the moment. Why on earth didn't you tell Dad, and ask his advice before you telephoned to Mr. Hicks?"

"That's a sensible thing for you to say," retorted Kit, hotly, "after you've all warned me not to worry Dad about anything. And I did not act upon impulse," she went on stiffly, "I made certain logical deductions from certain facts. How was I to know he was hunting

gypsy moths and other winged beasts when I
saw him bending over bushes in our berry
patch? Anyhow it would simplify matters if
Dad would let us know when he expected
visitors. You should have seen old Mr. Hicks'
face and Evie's, too. They were so disappointed
at not having a prisoner in tow to exhibit to
the Elmhurst populace on the way over to the
jail."

Mrs. Gorham glanced up over her glasses at
the circle of faces around the dining-room
table. The girls had volunteered to help her
pick over berries for canning the following day.
It was a sacrifice to make, too, with the mid-
summer evening calling to them—katydids
and peep frogs, the swish of the wind through
the big Norway pines on the terraces, and the
sound of Jack's harmonica from the back porch.
It was Friday evening, and Mr. and Mrs.
Craig had driven over to the Judge's for a
visit. Mr. Craig had invited the erstwhile
prisoner to accompany them, but he had decided instead to keep on his way to the old

Inn on the hill above the village, much to Jean
and Doris' disappointment.

Doris had discovered that his first name was
Frank, which relieved her mind considerably.

"If it had been Abijah or Silas, I know I
could never have forgiven him for getting in
the berry patch," she said, "but there is something promising about Frank."

"Wonder if I turned out that stove," Mrs.
Gorham said thoughtfully. "Seems like I smell
something. Tommy," she called raising her
voice, "will you see if I turned out that fire
under the syrup? I smell smoke."

"OK," called Tommy.

He got up slowly from his seat on the back
steps and sauntered into the kitchen. The
minute he walked in there poured out a spurt
of flame and smoke from the woodwork behind
the stove, and Tommy slammed the kitchen
door and ran for a pail.

It seemed incredible how fast the flames
spread. Summoned by his outcry, the girls
opened the door leading into the kitchen from

the dining room and quickly shut it again when they saw the flames. Tommy and Jack pulled the garden hose around to the back door and played the stream of water on the fire.

Mrs. Gorham made straight for the telephone, calling up the Judge, and two or three of the nearest neighbors for help. The Peckham boys from the sawmill were the first to respond, and five minutes later Matt was on the spot, having seen the rising smoke and flare in the sky from Maple Grove, Becky's old home.

"You'll never save the place," old Mr. Peckham told them flatly. "Everything is dry as tinder and the water pressure is low. Better start carrying things out, girls, because the best we can do is to keep the roofs wet down and try to save the barn."

While the fire was confined to the kitchen, the two older Peckham boys set to work upstairs, under Jean's direction. Kit had made for her father's room the first thing. When Jean opened the door she found her piling the contents of the desk and chest of drawers helter-skelter into blankets.

"It's OK, Jean," she called. "I'm not missing a thing. You tie the corners up and have the boys carry these downstairs and bring back the clothes basket and a couple of tubs for the books. Tell Doris to take the cat out of here."

"All right," answered Jean. "And Mrs. Gorham is getting all of the preserves out of the cellar, and Mr. Peckham says he's sure they'll save the piano and most of the best furniture, but, golly, Kit, just think of how Mom and Dad will feel when they see the flames in the sky, and know it's Woodhow burning."

"You'd better start in at mother's room and stop thinking, or we'll be sliding down a lightning rod to get out of here."

Nobody quite noticed Jack in the excitement, but later when all was over, it was found that he had rescued all the treasures possible, the pictures, all the linen and family silver, and the glassware.

As the rising glow of the flames lighted up the sky help began to arrive from all directions. Mrs. Gorham's thoughtfulness in telephoning immediately brought the Judge first, with all of the neighbors that had been at his home for the evening. Becky was bareheaded, little curly wisps of hair fluttering around her face.

"I made your father stay up at our place," she told them. "You'll all probably have to come back with me anyhow and excitement isn't good for him. Besides, he wouldn't be a bit of help around here. Seems like they're getting the fire under pretty good control. I don't believe all the house will go. It was so old anyway, and it needed to be rebuilt if you ever expect your great-grandchildren to live here."

Kit noticed an entirely new and unsuspected trait in Becky on this night of excitement. It was the only time when she had not seen her take command of the situation. But tonight she helped Mrs. Gorham pack all the necessary household supplies into the trailer for Matt to drive up to Maple Grove. As soon as she had seen the extent of the damage she had said immediately that the family must move up the hill to her own old home, where she had lived before her marriage to Judge Ellis.

"It won't take but a couple days to put it into shape for you, and Matt's right up there to look after things. You'll be back here before the snow flies, with a few modern improvements put in, and all of you the better for the change. Jack, go bring the family treasures from under that pine tree, and put them in the back of our car."

"You know, Becky," Kit exclaimed, "I thought the minute you showed up down here tonight you'd be the chief of the fire department."

Becky laughed. "Did you, dear? Well, I've always held that there are times and seasons when you ought to let the men alone. After you've lived a lifetime in these parts, you'll know that every boy born and bred around here is taught how to fight fire from the time he can tote a water bucket. Did you save all the chickens, Tommy?''

''Didn't lose even a guinea hen!'' Tommy assured her. ''The barn wasn't touched, and so I'm going to sleep over the harness room and watch the cow and her calf and the mare. Jack will stay too, and keep me company.''

3. The Important Letter

THE morning after the fire found the family at breakfast with the Judge's family. It was impossible as yet for the girls to feel the full reaction over their loss. Kit and Billie rode down before breakfast to look at the ruins, and came back with an encouraging report. The back of the house was badly damaged, but the main building stood intact, though the charred clapboards and wide vacant windows looked desolate enough.

"It was a good thing the wind was from the south and blew the flames away from the pines," said Kit, dropping into her chair at the table. "Doesn't it seem good to get some of

Becky's huckleberry pancakes again? Oh, yes, we met my prisoner on the road. He was tapping chestnut trees over on Peck's Hill like a woodpecker. You needn't laugh, Doris, 'cause Billie saw him too, didn't you, Bill? And he's got a sweet forgiving nature. He waved to me and I smiled back just as though I'd never caught him in our berry patch, and had Tommy lock him up in the corncrib."

"Was he heading this way?" the Judge asked. "I want him to look at my peach trees and tell me what ails them."

"Tom will be glad to go up with you to the peach orchard," put in Becky, "I want Jean and Kit and their mother to drive over and help fix Maple Grove."

The family had taken up its new quarters at Maple Grove before a week had passed, and two of the local carpenters, Mr. Horace Weaver, Philip's brother, and Mr. Delaplaine, had been persuaded to devote a portion of their valuable time to rehabilitating Woodhow. It took tact and persuasion to induce these men to desert their favorite chairs on the sidewalk in front of Byers' Grocery Store, and approach anything resembling daily toil. There had been a Squire in the Weaver family three generations back, and Horace held firmly to established precedent. He might be landed gentry, but he was no tiller of the soil, and he secretly looked down on his elder brother for personally cultivating the family acres.

Mr. Delaplaine was likewise addicted to reverie and historic retrospect. Nothing delighted Billie and Doris so much as to ride down to the store and get a chance to converse with both of the old men on local history. Mr. Delaplaine's mail, which consisted mostly of catalogues, came addressed to N. L. Delaplaine, Esq., but to Elmhurst he was just Niles Delaplaine.

Every day that first week found the girls and Tommy down at the old home prying around the ruins for any lost treasures. Frank Howard struck up a friendship with both the Judge and Mr. Craig, and usually drove by on his way from the village. He would stop and talk for a few minutes with them, but Kit was elusive. Vaguely, she felt that the proper thing for her to do was to offer an apology for even considering him an unlawful trespasser. When Frank would drive away, Jean would laugh at her teasingly.

"Gosh, why do you act so high and mighty? He seems very nice and he's awfully good-looking, even if he does chase caterpillars for a living. I never did see anyone but you, Kit, who hated to acknowledge herself in the wrong. The rest of us all have the most peaceful, forgiving sort of dispositions, but you can be a regular porcupine when you want to be."

"It could come from Uncle Bart," retorted Kit. "Did you hear them all talking about him over at the Judge's while we were there? Let's sit here under the pines a minute until the mailman goes by. I'm sick of poking over cinders. Becky said he was the only notable in our family. Dean Barton Cato Peabody. We ought to tell Mr. Delaplaine that."

"Sh-h," warned Jean, "he might hear you and it would hurt his feelings." She glanced back over her shoulder to where Mr. Delaplaine worked, taking off the outer layer of charred clapboards from the front of the house.

"Still it is nice to own a dean, almost as good as a squire," repeated Kit placidly.

"I didn't pay much attention to what they were saying about him," said Jean dreamily. "Is he still alive?"

"He is, but I guess he might as well be dead as far as the rest of the family is concerned. Becky said he'd never married, and he lived with his sister out in the middle west somewhere. Not the real west—I mean the interesting west like Saskatchewan and Saskatoon and—you know what I mean, Jean?"

Jean was particularly interested in Saskatoon for it was there that Ralph McRae lived. Ralph, who was twenty-five, had been the owner of Woodhow before the Craigs bought it and the first summer they were in Elmhurst, he had come to visit them and was immediately attracted to Jean. He had returned last spring with Buzzy Hancock, his cousin and a great friend of Kit's, who had spent the year with him. Then he had gone West again, taking Buzzy's sister, Sally, and Mrs. Hancock with him to make their home in Saskatoon. Jean missed him very much, more than she would admit to Kit or the others, and she looked forward to his frequent letters.

"There comes the mail," called Jean, starting up and running down the drive as the truck came in sight. The carrier waved a newspaper and letter at them.

"Nothing for you girls today, only a letter for your father and a weekly newspaper for Matt. I'll leave it up at the old place as I go by." He added as a happy afterthought to relieve any possible anxiety on their part, "It's from Delphi, Wisconsin."

Kit stood transfixed with wonder, as he passed on up the hill. "Jean," she said slowly, "there's something awfully queer about me.

That letter was from Uncle Barton Cato Peabody."

"Well, what if it is?" asked Jean, shaking the needles from her blouse.

"But, don't you get the significance? I was just telling you about him and now there's a letter from him for Dad."

4. Kit's Plan

IT APPEARED that Uncle Bart lived strictly up to tradition, for it had been over fifteen years since any word had been received from him. The letter which broke the long silence was read aloud several times that day, the girls and Tommy especially searching between its lines for any hidden sentiment or hint of family affection.

"I don't see why he tries to be generous when he doesn't know how," Doris said musingly. "I wonder if he's got bushy gray hair."

"Wait a minute while I read this thing over carefully again," Kit said. "I think while we're alone we ought to discuss it freely.

Mother just took it as if it were of no consequence. It seems to me, since it concerns us vitally, that we ought to have some selection in the matter ourselves.''

"But Kit, you didn't read carefully," Jean interrupted with a little laugh. "See here," she followed the writing with her fingertip. "He says, 'Send me the boy.' That means Tommy."

"Yes, I know it does, but Mom said she didn't want Tommy to go now. She said he's too young to go off alone."

"Well then, that scotches the deal as far as the rest of us are concerned."

"I don't see why I can't go," said Kit rather sadly. "I should have been a boy anyway, I'm more like Dad than any of you."

"No matter what you say," Jean replied, "I don't think you're especially like Dad at all. He hasn't a quick temper and he's not the least bit domineering."

Kit leaned over her tenderly. "Darling, am I domineering to you? Have I crushed your spirit? I'm awfully sorry. I didn't mean that my bad habits were inherited from Dad. What I meant was my initiative and craving for something new and different. Just at the moment I can't think of anything that would be more interesting or adventurous than going out to Uncle Bart's, and trying to fulfill all his expectations."

"Thought you wanted to go out to the Alameda Ranch with Uncle Hal more than anything in the world, a little while ago. You're forever changing your mind, Kit."

"Golly, I wouldn't give a darn for a person who couldn't face new emergencies and feel within them the surge of—of—"

"We admit the surge, but would you really and truly be willing to go to this place? I don't even know what state it's in."

There was a footstep in the long hallway, and Mr. Craig came into the living room.

"Dad," called Doris, "were you ever in Delphi, where Uncle Bart lives?"

Mr. Craig sat down on the arm of Jean's chair and lit his pipe.

"Just once, long ago when I was about eight years old. We, that is, my mother and I, stayed for about a week at Delphi. It's a little college town on Lake Michigan, perhaps sixty miles north of Chicago on the big bluffs that line the shore nearly all the way to Milwaukee. Uncle Bart helped to establish Hope College there in Wisconsin. I don't remember so very much about it, though, it was so long ago. I seem to remember Uncle Bart's house was rather cheerless and formal. He was a good deal of a scholar and antiquarian. Aunt Della seemed to me just a little shadow that followed after him, and made life smooth."

Kit listened very closely to every word he said, and Jean was looking up at him seriously.

"I don't think," continued their father easily, "that it would be a very cheerful or sympathetic home for any young person. Your mother is right in not wanting to let Tommy go."

"Oh, but Dad, gee," Kit burst out eagerly, "Think what a challenge it would be to make them understand how much more interesting you can make life if you only take the right point of view.''

"Yes, but supposing what seemed to be the right point of view to you, Kit, was not the right point of view to them at all. Everyone looks at life from his own angle.''

"Aldo always said that, too," Jean put in. "Remember, the boy from Italy I met when I was in New York last winter? I remember at our art class each student would see the subject from a different angle and sketch accordingly. Aldo said it was exactly like life, where each one gets his own perspective.''

"But you can't get any perspective at all if you shut yourself up in the dark," Kit argued. She leaned her chin on her hands. "Now just listen to this, and don't all speak at once until I get through. You went away, Jean, to New York, and though maybe I shouldn't say this, you came back home very much better satisfied and pleasanter to live with. I think after you've stayed in one place too long you get fed up and wish there were some way to get away somewhere. I haven't any special talent for art or anything like that, but I'd like to get away and see something different for a change. And Dad darling, if you would only consent to let me go for even two or three months, I will come back to you a perfect angel, besides doing Uncle Bart and Aunt Della oodles of good."

"It sounds right enough, dear," Mr. Craig said, his gray eyes full of amusement, "but we can't very well disguise you as a boy, and Uncle Bart is not the kind of person to trifle with."

Kit thought this over seriously.

"Don't tell them until I've started," she suggested, "and be sure and mail the letter so it will get there after I do, and send me quick, so they won't have any chance to change their minds. Jean will be here and you really and truly don't need me here at all."

"Well, I don't know what to say, Kit. I'll have to talk it over with your mother first. I wonder why Uncle Bart wanted Tommy specially."

"Maybe he thought a boy would be more interested in antiques. Are they Chinese porcelains and jewels, or just mummy things?"

"Mostly ruins, as I remember," laughed her father. "When he was young, Uncle Bart used to be sent away by the Geographical Society to explore buried cities in Chaldea and Egypt."

"I wish I could coax him to start in again, right now, and take me with him," Kit exclaimed, blithely. "Anyhow, I'm going to hope that it will come right and I can go. Can I borrow your trunk Jean? Just write a charming letter, Dad, sort of in the abstract, thanking him and calling us 'the children' so he can't detect just what we are, then when I depart, you can wire them, 'Kit arrives such and such a time.' They'll probably expect a Christopher, and once I land there, and they realize the treasure you have sent them, they will forgive me anything."

Uncle Bart's letter was read over again carefully by Mrs. Craig. Kit carried it out to the grape arbor where she was shelling peas for dinner.

"Just read that letter over, Mom, very, very carefully, and see if there isn't some way you can smuggle me out to Delphi, without hurting Uncle Bart's feelings."

Mrs. Craig took the letter and together they read it again—

My dear Thomas:

I trust both you and Margaret are enjoying good health, and that this finds you both facing a more prosperous time than when I heard last from you.

It has occurred to both Della and myself that we may be able to relieve you of part of your responsibility and care, at least for a short time. If the experiment should prove advantageous to all concerned we might be able to arrange a longer stay. One suggestion, however, I feel privileged to make. We would prefer that you would send the boy, as you know this is a college town, and I am sure it would broaden his views to come west, even for a short time. I need hardly add that we will do all in our power to make his stay a pleasant and profitable one.

Another point to consider is this. I would like to interest him in a few of my little hobbies, archaeology, geology, etc. I have delved deeply into the mysteries of the past, and feel I should pass on what I have learned as a heritage to youth.

Trusting that you and Margaret will be able to coincide with our views in the matter, I remain,

Yours faithfully,
Barton C. Peabody.

"You know, Mom," here Kit slipped her arm persuasively around her mother's shoulder, "you've always said yourself that I was more like a boy. And Buzzy says I'm an awfully good pal, and he'd much rather talk to me than any of the boys around here because I understand what he's driving at."

"I don't think it would matter, if you only visited them for a couple of months, but supposing Uncle Bart took a fancy to you." Mrs. Craig's eyes twinkled as she watched Kit's grave face.

"You mean," she said, "supposing he decided that my brain measured up to his expectation and they wanted me to stay all winter? Couldn't I go to school there, just as well as here? You ought to realize, Mom, that I'm really not a child any longer. I'm sixteen."

"Reaching years of discretion, aren't you," smiled her mother. "I suppose it would do you a lot of good in a broadening way to go through a new experience like this."

"I'm not thinking about that." Kit sent back an understanding gleam of fun, "but I'm perfectly positive that it would do Uncle Bart and Aunt Della an awful lot of good."

"Then we shouldn't deprive them of the opportunity. Do you think so, Matt?"

Matt stuck his head through the vines and clustering leaves. "Couldn't do no harm either way, s'far as I can see," he said. "And if the old.folks need any sort of discipline, I'd certainly start Miss Kit after them."

5. Farewell Party

THAT was the end of August. Becky approved of the plan, and said no doubt the fire down at Woodhow had been a good thing after all.

"You were all of you settling down into a rut before it happened, and the old place needed a thorough going over anyhow. You know you couldn't have afforded it, Tom, if it hadn't been for the fire insurance money coming in so handy. Now, you'll all move back the first part of the winter, with the new furnace set up, and no cracks for the wind to whistle through. Jean will be here and I don't think Kit's a bit too young to be going off alone. Land alive, Margaret, you ought to be

47

so thankful that you've got children with any get-up to them in this day and age. The Judge and I were saying just the other night it seems as if most of the young people up around here haven't got any pluck or initiative at all. They're born to feel that they're heirs of grace, and most of them are sure of having a farm or wood lot in their own right, sooner or later.''

So the trunk stood open most of the time, and Kit prepared for her trip to Delphi. Mr. Craig was inclined to take it as rather a good joke on the Dean, but Mrs. Craig could not get over a certain little feeling of conscience in the matter. The rest of the family pinned its faith on Kit's persuasive adaptability.

Tommy was a little disappointed at first not to be going, but then he thought of leaving Jack behind. He knew that Jack would be sure to get into trouble if he weren't there to look after him and he was extremely proud of his responsibility. Doris dreaded going back to school without Kit.

''Lucy Peckham will go over with you,''

Kit told her cheerfully, "and just think of the wonderful letters you'll have from me, Doris. Miss Cogswell says that I always shine best when I'm writing, and I'll tell you all the news of Hope College. By the way, Dad told me last night that he's pretty sure in those little family colleges they run a prep department, which takes in the last two years of high school. Perhaps I could persuade them that the great-grandniece of Barton Cato would be a deserving object of their consideration. Don't forget to pack my skates, Doris. I let you have them last, and they're hanging in your closet."

Becky decided to have a farewell party, two nights before Kit left, and the girls and Tommy were delighted. Any party launched by Becky promised novelty and excitement.

They danced in the living room to the tune of the records on the phonograph. In the library, some of the younger ones were playing forfeits. Abby Tucker was giving out forfeits, sitting blindfolded on a chair.

It happened that Doris's little turquoise for-

get-me-not ring was the particular forfeit dang-
ling over Abby's head, when Billie stuck his
head in at the open window, and Abby lifted
her chin at the sound of his voice.

"She must catch Billie Ellis, and bring him
back to kneel at my feet, and hand over his
forfeit."

Billie had evaded this, whirling about in the
driveway and speeding down the long lane
with Doris in fast pursuit. Overhead the mul-
berry trees met in a leafy arcade, and out of the
hazel thicket a whippoorwill called, flying
low down the lane after the two darting forms,
as if it were trying to find out what the excitement was about at that time of night. At the
turn of the lane there were three apple trees,
early Shepherd Sweetings, and here Billie
slipped down and lay breathing heavily, his
hands hunting for windfalls in the tall grass.
Doris passed him by, speeding the full length
of the lane and bringing up at the end of the log
run before the old mill.

"Billie Ellis, you come out of there," she

called. "I've got my shoes wet already chasing after you, and I'm not going to climb all over those old timbers hunting for you."

Only the whippoorwill answered, calling now from a clump of elderberry bushes close by the water's edge, and while she stood listening, there was the dull splash in the pond where some big bullfrog had taken alarm at her coming.

Billie gathered a goodly supply of apples, and stole after her in the shadows.

"Well, I'm not going to stay out here all night waiting for you," Doris said, addressing the wide dark entrance to the mill, when all at once there came his voice, directly behind her shoulder.

"Why didn't you try to catch me? I was resting back under the apple tree. Let's sit down over the falls and eat some apples. If Abby's waiting for me to kneel in front of her, she'll wait all night. I'd like to see myself kneeling in front of a girl!"

The words had hardly left his lips, before

Doris played an old-time schoolgirl trick on him. Catching him by his collar, she twirled him about with an odd twist until he knelt in front of her. Although Billie was older than she was, she had managed to catch him off guard. Billie shook himself ruefully when he rose.

"You always catch a guy when he's not expecting anything," he said.

"Do you good," she retorted serenely. "Ever since you went away to school, you've had a high and mighty opinion of yourself. I hope you get over it. Aren't these apples swell, though? Do you suppose they'll mind very much if we stay just a few minutes? Don't you love this old pond, Bill? Remember your flat-bottomed boat that always leaked when we used to go fishing in it. How I hated to take turns bailing it out."

"Yeah. Gee, I wish I didn't have to go back to school so soon."

"Wouldn't it be strange, Bill, if either of us were famous some day? I know you're going to be somebody special. Maybe it will be in natural history."

Billie laughed comfortably, perching himself just below her on the heavy timbers of the old sluice gate. "Grandfather says I have a great responsibility on my shoulders, because I'm the last of the Ellis family. He says there's always been an Ellis in the State Legislature at Hartford, ever since there was a legislature, and just as soon as I'm old enough, he's going to send me to law school. Gee, I wish he wouldn't. Think of being shut up all day long in an office."

Far down the lane they heard the others calling them and Doris sprang up, scattering apples as she did so.

"I'd forgotten all about the party," she exclaimed. "Anyway, I'm glad we had a chance to talk. If I were you, I'd just read and study everything I could lay my hands on about insects and things, all the time I was in school, and then when the Judge sees that you're in dead earnest about it, he'll let you go on. I heard Dad say that Mr. Howard knew more about insects than any man he'd ever met, and that he was considered one of the coming experts in government work. Why, Bill, it's just like a great scientist or doctor, who is able to discover a certain germ that can be used as a toxin, only you doctor plants and things."

"I know," Billie agreed enthusiastically. "There's some man who discovered the cause of the wheat blight in the south and somebody else figuring out what was killing our chestnuts off. Doris, you're a swell pal. If it wasn't for you, I don't know whether I'd ever have seen a chance to study what I want to, but you encourage me."

Doris laughed and tagged him on the shoulder as she broke into a run. "You're it. Don't give anyone else the credit for starting you off in the way you know you ought to go. Just take a deep breath and race for it."

6. "The Boy's" Arrival

Mr. Craig had answered the first letter from Delphi, under Kit's careful supervision, and the acceptance was vague enough to please her.

It aroused no suspicions whatever in the minds of Dean Peabody or Aunt Della. The only question was, who was to meet the child in Chicago. The through express would leave *him* there, and in order to connect with the Wisconsin trains it was necessary to make the change over to the Northwestern Depot.

Della was far more perturbed over it than her brother. Having set in motion the coming guest, he believed firmly that an unfaltering Fate would direct his footsteps safely to

Delphi. Barton Cato Peabody had been peculiar all his life. He had been a strange boy, unsettled, studious, impractical. Miss Della was his younger sister, and ever since her youth had tried to give him all the love and encouragement that others refused. She had followed him faithfully and happily on all of his exploring expeditions. Perhaps one reason why these had been so successful was because she had always managed to surround him with home comforts, even in the wilds of the upper Nile.

And perhaps the quaintest thing about it all was that Della herself, no matter on what particular point of the globe she had happened to pitch her tent, had always retained her courage, although she had faced dangers that the average woman would have fled from.

Their house stood on the same hill as Hope College, the highest point in the rising ridge of bluffs along the Lake Shore at Delphi. It was built of dark red brick, a square house with long French windows. A grove of pine trees almost hid it from view on its street side, the stately Norway pines that Kit loved. The back of the house looked directly out over the lake, and the land here was frankly left to nature. Trees, grass, and underbrush rioted at will, until they suddenly ended on the brow of the bluff, where there was a sheer drop to the beach. Looking at it from below, Kit afterwards thought it was like a miniature section of the Yosemite; the sand had hardened into fantastic shapes, and the rock strata in places was plainly visible.

Mrs. Craig's telegram arrived the night before Kit herself. It was brief and noncommittal. "Kit arrives Union Station, Chicago, Thursday, 10:22 A.M."

"Kit," repeated the Dean. "Humph! Nickname. Superfluous and derogatory."

Della took the telegram from his desk with a little smile that was almost tremulous with excitement. "It's probably the diminutive for Christopher, Bart," she said. "I think it's a nice name. I always liked the legend of St. Christopher. Somebody'll have to meet him down in Chicago. He might lose his head and take the wrong train."

"He's about sixteen, isn't he? Old enough to change from one train to another, and use his tongue if he's in doubt. When I was sixteen, Della, I was earning my own living working on a farm summers, and going to a school in the winter where we all had to work for our board. Never hurt us a bit. The greatest trait of character you can instill in a child is self-reliance."

Della had a little way of appearing to listen while her brother expounded on any of his favorite subjects. It had grown to be a habit with her, and she had a way of answering absently, "Yes, dear, I'm quite sure of it," which always satisfied him that he had her attention. But now, she sat looking out the window and thinking, a perplexed expression on her face.

It had not altogether been her desire that the coming child should be a boy, although not one word had she breathed of this to Dean

Peabody. The determination to take one of the Craig children had been a sudden one. The Dean had been reading somebody's theory about the obligations of age to youth.

"Della, my dear," he had remarked one evening, as the two sat quietly in the old library, "we have been leading very narrow, selfish lives, and we will suffer for it as we grow older. We have shut ourselves away from youth. I am seventy-four now, and what heritage am I leaving to the world beyond a few books of reference, and my collections? What I should do is to take some child, still in the impressionable stage, and impart to it all I know."

Della glanced up with a little amused twinkle in her eyes. "But, Bart, what about the child? Surely you would require an exceptional child for such an experiment. One who would have the mentality to grasp all that you were trying to impart to it."

The Dean thought this over, pursing his lips and tapping his knuckles with his rimless glasses. "Possibly," he granted, "and yet, Della, surely there would be far more credit attached to planting the seed of knowledge where it needed much cultivating. It has surprised and amazed me up at the college to find that usually the children who appreciate an education are the farmer boys, and very often the foreign element."

Della rocked to and fro gently. She knew her brother well enough to understand that this had become a fixed idea with him, and the easiest way out was to find him an impressionable child. And then, it happened that she thought of Thomas Craig, their nephew, and all his children. She remembered having one letter after the breaking up of the home on Long Island.

"You know what I think, Bart," began Della in the bright, abrupt way she had, "I think it would be the right thing if we took one of the Craig children. There are four or five of them—"

"Boys or girls?" interrupted the Dean.

"Well, now I'm not quite sure, but if my memory serves me, I think there's a boy among them. I know the eldest one is a girl. They're all of them over ten, I'm sure. Why don't you just write to Thomas and make known your willingness? I am sure they would take it in the spirit in which it was offered."

So this was how it happened that the Dean's letter went forth to Elmhurst, and produced the hour when Kit stood on the platform of the Union Station in Chicago, looking around her to discover anyone who might appear to be seeking a small boy.

Gradually the long platform that led up to the concourse cleared. Kit went slowly on, following the porter who carried her suitcase. She was looking for someone who might resemble either the Dean or Della from her father's description of them.

"As I remember him," Mr. Craig had said, "the Dean was very tall, rather sparely built, but broad-shouldered and always with his head up to the wind. His hair was gray and curly. Aunt Della was like a little bird, a gentle, plump, busy woman, with bright brown eyes and a little smile that never left her lips. I am sure you can't mistake them, Kit, for in their way they are very distinctive.''

Yet Kit was positive now that neither the Dean nor his sister had come to meet her. She stood in the waiting room wearing a dark brown gabardine coat with a brown hat to match. There was about her an air of buoyant and friendly self-possession, which always endeared her to even casual acquaintances. Therefore it was no wonder that Rex Bellamy glanced at her several times with interest, even while his gaze sought through the crowd for a young New England boy, bound for Delphi, Wisconsin.

But Kit noticed Rex Bellamy. Noticed his alert anxiety as he walked up and down, eyeing every newcomer. He was eighteen or nineteen, and unmistakably looking for someone. Even while Kit watched, she saw a girl of about her own age hurry up to him. Her voice reached Kit plainly, as she said, "I've looked up and down that end, and I'm positive he isn't there. Oh, but the Dean will lecture you, Rex, if you miss him."

At this identical moment, Rex's eyes met a pair of dancing, mischievous ones, and Kit crossed over to where they stood.

"I do believe you must be looking for me," she said. "I'm Kit Craig."

"Oh, but we were expecting your brother," exclaimed the other girl, eagerly.

"I know, but you see my brother's only twelve," said Kit, "and the family thought he was too young to come. I begged to come instead. I'm afraid the Dean made a little mistake, didn't he? Do you think he'll mind so very much when he sees me?"

"Mind?" repeated Rex. "Why, I think he'll be perfectly delighted. My name is Rex Bellamy, Kit, and this is my sister, Anne. We're next-door neighbors of the Dean and Miss

Della, and as we happened to be coming in town today they asked us to be sure to meet your—'' Here he hesitated.

"My brother," laughed Kit. "Well, here I am, and I only hope that Mother's letter reached them this morning, explaining everything. Of course, they did write for a boy, and it takes so long for a letter to get out here and be answered, that I told Mom and Dad I knew it would be perfectly all right for me to come instead. Don't you think it will be?''

Anne's blue eyes were full of merriment. "Oh, golly," she exclaimed, "I do wish I could go back with you, so I could see their faces when they find out. Mother and I have been here in Chicago this summer and Rex has been living at home alone. We'll be back in a week, so I'll see you then, and anyway, we're sure to visit back and forth. I'm awfully glad you're a girl.''

"But I won't be here all winter," Kit answered. "I've only come for a couple of months. On trial, you see. Maybe it'll be only a couple of days, if they're terribly disappointed." Anne exchanged quick glances with her brother and he smiled as he led the way to the car.

"You don't know the elaborate plans the Dean has laid out for your education," he said. "It will take you all winter long to live up to them, but I'm sure he won't be disappointed."

Kit had her own opinion about this, still it was impossible for her to feel apprehensive or unhappy, as the car sped over toward the Lake Shore Drive. The newness of everything after two years up in the Elmhurst hills was wonderfully stimulating. But it was not until they had left the city and river behind and had reached Lincoln Park that she really gave vent to her feelings. It was a wonderful day and the lake lay in sparkling ripples beyond the long stretch of shore.

"Are we going all the way in the car?" she asked.

Rex shook his head. "No, only as far as

Evanston. We'll drop Anne off, and have lunch with Mother and then catch the train to Delphi. I have an errand for the Dean out at the University.''

"Gee," said Kit, "we lived right on the edge of Long Island Sound before we moved up to Connecticut, and ever since I was small I can remember going away somewhere to the seashore every summer, but I think your lake is ever so much more interesting than the ocean. Somehow it seems to belong to you more. I always felt with the ocean as if it just condescended to come over to my special beach, after it had rambled all over the world, and belonged to everybody.''

"But you have all the shells and the seaweed, and we haven't," argued Anne. "Before I ever went East, we had a couple of clam shells, just plain everyday round clam shells that had come from Cape May, and I used to think they were perfectly wonderful because they had belonged in the real ocean.''

After the rugged landscape of New England,

Kit found this level land very attractive. They passed through one suburb after another, with the beautiful Drive following the curving shoreline out to Evanston. Here she caught her first glimpse of Northwestern University, its buildings showing picturesquely through the beautiful trees around the campus.

They left Rex at the main entrance and drove on to where Mrs. Bellamy was stopping. Mrs. Bellamy was filled with amusement when she heard the story of Kit's substitution of herself for her brother that the Dean had asked for. She was a tall, slender woman with blonde hair and gray eyes, who seemed almost like an older sister of Anne's. They were staying in a small apartment near the campus.

Early in the afternoon Rex returned, and they caught the 2:45 local to Delphi. Kit could hardly keep her eyes off the beautiful scenery they were passing through. Every now and then the rich blueness of the lake would flash through the trees in the distance, and to the west there stretched long level fields of prairie land, dipping ravines that un-expectedly led into woodland. Gradually the bluffs heightened as they neared the Wisconsin line above Waukegan, and just beyond the state line, between the shore and the region of the small lakes, Oconomowoc and Delevan, they came suddenly upon Delphi. It stood high upon the bluff, its college dominating the shady serenity of its quiet avenues.

"The Dean doesn't keep a car," said Rex as they walked through the gray stone station. "Besides, he thought I was bringing a boy who would not mind the hike up the hill."

"I don't mind a bit," replied Kit. "I like it. It seems good to find real hills after all. I thought everything out here was just flat. I do hope they won't be watching for us. It will be ever so much easier if I can just walk in before they get any kind of a shock, don't you think?"

Rex did not tell her which was the house until they came to the two tall poplars at the entrance to the drive. Kit caught the murmur of the waves as they broke on the shore below and lifted her chin eagerly.

"Oh, I like it," she cried. "This is it, isn't it? Isn't it dreamy? I only hope they'll let me stay."

7. The House Under the Bluff

DEAR FAMILY,

I can't stop to write separate letters to-night to all of you, because I'm so full of Delphi that I can hardly think of anything else. First of all, Rex met me at the train with his sister Anne. They live next door and Rex is Uncle Bart's pet educational proposition next to me.

Mother's letter had not arrived and they were expecting Tommy any moment, when Rex and I walked in on them, and right here I must say they showed presence of mind. The Dean's eyes twinkled as Rex explained things, and then I kissed Aunt Della, and explained to her too, and I'm sure that she was relieved. After Rex had gone, the Dean took me into his study after dinner, and we had a long heart-to-heart talk. I want you all to understand that he thinks I'm a good specimen of the undeveloped female brain.

I am going to enter the preparatory class at the college in October, and take what the Dean calls supplementary lessons from him along special lines. I don't quite know all that this means, but I guess I can weather it. It probably has to do with cosmic makings (those were Rex's words) of geology and all sorts of prehistoric stuff. I know the Dean mentioned one thing that began with a 'paleo' but I have forgotten the rest of it. I'll let you know later.

I have a perfectly darling room. It looks right out over Lake Michigan. There's a big square window to it that overhangs

the edge of the bluff like the balcony of a
Spanish villa. Our garden just topples right
over into a ravine that ends up short on
the shore. I never saw such abrupt cliffs in
my life. Uncle Bart was showing me the
layers of strata there that a little recent
landslide had shown up, and he says that
the formation is just exactly like it is out
in Wyoming and Colorado.

Aunt Della is darling. It's more fun to
hear her tell of how she worried over a boy
coming into the family. The whole house
is filled from one end to the other with
Uncle Bart's treasures that he's been col-
lecting for years. You're liable to stumble
over a stuffed armadillo or a petrified slice
of some prehistoric monster anywhere at
all. I found a mummy case in the library
closet, but there wasn't anything in itat
all, and I was awfully disappointed. I don't
know but what I like it after all, although
I miss you dreadfully. I don't even dare to

think there are about a thousand miles between us.

So I won't feel too out of touch with all of you, you must promise to write me often. Jean, I want you to tell me all that you hear from Ralph. I strongly suspect something is going on between you two, even though you haven't said anything about it to me. We always talked things over together before, so now that I'm away we'll have to do the discussing by letter.

Doris, be sure to keep me posted on all the things you are doing at school, and, Tommy, you are to give me the details on the progress of rebuilding Woodhow.

If you will do this, I know I'll feel as if I'm right there at home and I won't be homesick at all.

This is all I can write to you tonight because I'm so sleepy I can hardly keep my eyes open. Aunt Della was just in to say good night. She told me again how glad she is that I'm not a boy. Uncle Bart hasn't committed himself yet, but I think he's curious about me anyway. Good night all, and write me oodles of news.

Love,
Kit.

At the same time that Kit was writing home, the Dean and Della stepped out on the broad porch. Every evening about nine-thirty passersby might have seen the flickering glow of the Dean's good-night cigar. His evening cigar was a sort of nocturnal ceremonial. It gave him an excuse to step out into the fragrant darkness of the garden walk for a quiet little stroll before bedtime, and usually Della joined him.

So tonight they walked together, discussing the girl with the dark curls who had come to them from far-off New England, instead of the boy they had sent for.

"There's no reason," remarked the Dean reflectively, "why the child should not have a pleasant visit, since she is here. I have had a long conversation with her, and while I could not say that she was exceptionally—er—"

"Bright," suggested Della.

"I should like to call it intellectual," the Dean said kindly, "she is keenly impressionable and self-reliant. I think I may be able to interest her, at least in a simplified course of study. I have always believed that boys were more able to accept routine discipline in education than girls, but we shall see."

Della's eyes, if he could only have seen them, held a twinkle of mirth, and her smile was a little more pronounced than usual.

"I think," she said, softly, "that she is a very lovable, attractive girl. I am quite relieved, Barton, not to have a boy in the house."

Kit woke up the following morning with the sunlight calling to her. It was early, but back on the farm she usually got up about six. There did not seem to be anyone stirring yet, so she dressed quietly, and found her way downstairs. The Dean kept a cook and gar-

dener. Kit heard Carrie, the cook, singing in
the dining room and went out at once to make
friends with her.

"Is it very far down the bluff to the shore,
Carrie?" she asked, eagerly. "I'm dying to
climb down there, if I have time before breakfast."

"Sure, Miss, it's as easy as rolling off a log.
You take the roundabout way through the
garden, and the little path behind the tool
shed, and you just follow it until you can't go
any farther, and there's the bluff. I haven't
been down myself, but Dan says there's a little
path you take to the shore if you don't mind
scrambling a bit."

Kit waved goodbye to her and went in search
of the path. She found Dan, the gardener, rak-
ing up leaves in the garden. He was a plump,
rosy-cheeked old Irishman, his face wrinkled
like a winter apple, and he lifted his cap at her
approach with a smile of frank curiosity and
approval.

A half-grown black retriever came bounding

to meet her, his nose and forepaws tipped with white.

"That's a welcome he's giving you you wouldn't have had if you'd been a boy, Miss," Dan said shrewdly. "I'm glad to meet you and hope you'll like it here."

Kit was stroking Sandy's head. His real name, Dan told her, was Lysander. Anything that the Dean had the naming of received the benediction of ancient Greece, but Sandy, in his puppyhood, had managed to acquire a happy nickname.

"I don't see," Kit said laughing, "why you dreaded a boy coming. I know some awfully nice boys back home, and there's one especially, named Buzzy. He's out West now. I think he's just the kind of a boy the Dean expected to see, but perhaps he'll get used to me. Do you think he will?"

"Sure he will," answered Dan. "If you leave it to Sandy to find the shore, he'll take you the quickest way."

Everything was so different from the Connecticut countryside. Instead of the thick, lush growth which came from richly watered black loam, here one found sand cherries and dwarf willows and beeches springing up from the sand. Tall sword grass waved almost like Becky's striped ribbon grass in her home garden, and wild sunflowers showed like golden glow here and there.

The beach was level and rockless, different entirely from the Eastern Atlantic shores, but the sand was beautifully white and fine, and there were great weatherbeaten, wave-washed boulders lying half-buried in the sand, also trunks of trees, their roots sticking out grotesquely like the heads of strange animals. Kit thought to herself how the Dean might have added them with profit to his prehistoric collection. There was no glimpse or hint of the town to be seen down here. Not even a boathouse, only one long pier. About a mile and a half from shore was a lighthouse, and farther out a dark freighter showed in perfect outline against the blueness of the morning sky.

Kit followed Sandy's lead, hardly realizing the distance she was covering, until he suddenly disappeared behind a headland. When she rounded it, she saw a cottage built close under the shelter of the bluff. The sand drifted like snow halfway up to its windows. It had been painted red once, but now its old clapboards were the color of sorrel, and weather-beaten and wave-washed like the boulders. There were fish nets drying on tall staples driven in behind a couple of overturned rowboats, and at that first glimpse it seemed to her as if there were children everywhere. Four strong boys from fourteen to eighteen worked over the nets, mending them. Around the back door there were four or five more, and sitting in the sunlight in a low rocking chair was an old woman.

Sandy seemed to greet them as old acquaintances, so Kit called good morning in her friendly way. The boys eyed her, and all of the children scurried like a flock of startled chickens as she came up the boardwalk to the kitchen door, but the old grandmother kept serenely on paring potatoes, calm-eyed and un-embarrassed.

"How do you do?" said Kit, and she smiled. "I'm Dean Peabody's grandniece. I just came here yesterday, and Sandy brought me here this morning. I didn't know where he was going, but he seemed to know the way."

The old woman's brown eyes followed the movement of the dog. "He's very fine, that dog," she said deliberately. "He comes very often, I've known him since he was *un petit chien*, very small pup—so big." She measured with her hand from the ground.

"Do you know the Dean?" Kit asked, sitting down on the doorstep beside her. "He lives up in the big house on the bluff, where the pine and maples are."

The old woman shook her head placidly. "I not go up that bluff in forty-eight years."

Kit's eyes widened with quick interest. Just then a girl a little older than herself came out of the kitchen door. Two pigtails of straight brown hair hung to her shoulders, and her dress was gypsy-like. She looked at Kit with quiet, steady scrutiny, and then questioningly over at the boys. But Kit herself relieved the tension.

"Hi," she said. "I think you've got an awfully nice place down here. I like it because it looks old like our houses back home. All the other places I've seen since I came out here have looked so newly-painted."

"This isn't new," the girl told her slowly. "This place belonged to my grandfather's father, Charles Flambeau. There were Indians around here then. Most of them Ojibways."

Kit's curiosity was aroused by this entirely new field of adventure to be uncovered. The wonderful old grandmother, basking in the sun with memories of the past. The strong, tanned boys working at the nets, the flock of dark-skinned youngsters, and the girl, Jeannette, whom she was to know so well before her stay in Delphi was over.

She hurried back, eager to ask questions

about the Flambeaus, and found herself late for breakfast the very first morning she was there. The Dean's face was a study as she entered, and Della's fingers fluttered nervously over the coffee pot and cups. Kit was out of breath, and so full of excitement that she did not even notice the air was chill.

"I've had a perfectly wonderful time," she began. "No coffee, Aunt Della, please. It's all Sandy's fault. I just wanted to run down the bluff to the shore, and he led me way around that headland to the quaintest old house, half-sunken in the sand, and I got acquainted with the old grandmother and Jeannette. The boys and the little kids seemed half-scared to death at the sight of me, and so I didn't bother to get acquainted with them yet."

The Dean looked up at her over his glasses with a quizzical expression, and Della fairly caught her breath.

"The Flambeaus on the shore, my dear?" she asked. "Those half-breed French Canadians?"

"Well, I didn't know just what they were," answered Kit cheerfully, "but I think they're awfully interesting. Don't you think that they look like the Breton fishermen in some of the old French paintings?"

"The Flambeaus have not a very good reputation, my dear," the Dean coughed slightly behind his hand as he spoke. "The present generation may be law-abiding, but even within my memory, the Flambeaus had a little habit of stealing."

"Stealing?" repeated Kit.

"Yes, fishing tackle and that sort of thing. Besides, there is the Indian strain in them, and they are squatters. There have been several lawsuits against them, and they have persisted in staying there on the shore when the property owners on the bluff distinctly purchased shore rights."

"But, Bart, the Flambeaus won all their suits, didn't they?" asked Della pleasantly. "I'm sure the older boys are very industrious, and I think the girl Jeanette is strikingly attractive. You're not really forbidding Kit to go down there, I'm sure."

The Dean said something that was lost in a murmur, for he had been one of the property owners defeated in the lawsuits by the Flambeaus. After breakfast Kit went upstairs with Della into her own little sitting room. This looked toward the street, out over the maple and pine-shaded lawn. Also, it commanded a good view of the college. This was built of gray stone and was overgrown with woodbine just beginning to show a tinge of crimson.

"It seems awfully queer, Aunt Della," Kit said as she leaned out of the window, "to think that I'm going there into the prep class. Rex said on the way up here—"

She leaned suddenly farther out and waved. "Hi, Rex, are you coming over?"

Rex glanced up at the radiant face as he came along the hedge-bordered drive between his home and the Dean's and waved back in neighborly fashion.

"I'm going up to the campus now," he said.

"Ask Miss Della if she'd let you be in the dramatic club. There's a meeting this morning."

"Could I, Aunt Della? Please say yes. I'm dying to join something. I haven't joined anything in ages," Kit begged. "I can meet everyone and get acquainted. If you don't need me this morning—" She hesitated, but some of her enthusiasm had caught Della, and she immediately succumbed to the whim of the moment.

"Why, I don't see why not. You go on down with Rex if you want to."

The Dean's desk stood overlooking the driveway. He had settled down to his morning's portion of work and was blocking out a curriculum of study for Kit, when he happened to glance up, and saw the two passing gayly through the gates. Certainly he did not realize at that moment that already the spirit of youth was at work in the old shadowy house behind the pines.

8. A Square Deal

THE first batch of family letters arrived the following week. Kit nearly knocked the mailman over as he came up the walk, for she had been watching anxiously at each delivery. After all, it was the first time she had been away from home, and after the first excitement and novelty had worn off, her heart ached for news from home.

It seemed the Dean had written to her father on the night of her arrival, and this was a surprise to Kit.

"It is a great relief to us all to know that

you have made such a favorable impression," Mr. Craig's letter read. "After all, it was an experiment, and I confess that I was rather skeptical of the result, knowing the Dean as I do. Try to adapt yourself as much as possible to their life there, Kit. You must be considerate of all the Dean's notions, and make yourself as useful as you can while you are with them.

"The rebuilding of the house is going along splendidly, and we hope to have our Christmas there. I have followed the old plan, but with some improvements, I think, putting in a good furnace, and enlarging the dining room and kitchen. There will be an outdoor fireplace on the west side of the house also, and I know you will enjoy this."

Enjoy it? Kit stared ahead of her at the shady lawn. Della was bending over nasturtium beds gathering black seeds, but instead, Kit saw in a vision a great hickory fire burning brightly against a black sky. Her mother's letter came next. Kit read it with delight. She could tell just exactly the mood her mother was in when she wrote, just how her conscience pricked her for having been a party to Kit's plan.

"Of course, while the Dean's letter was very nice, still I am sure he felt put upon. I am ever so sorry that we did not write sooner, and tell them that you were coming. It rests with you now, Kit, to make yourself so adaptable that they will forget all about wanting a boy. I have no objection to your staying for the winter term at Hope College. Between ourselves, dear, our plans are a little unsettled. Dad is certain that the house will be ready for us this winter, but you know how slowly the carpenters work.

"Make all the friends that you possibly can. You won't realize it now, but so many of these friendships become precious lifelong ones. Billie is leaving this week for school. You remember Frank Howard, who came to look after our trees? He has been staying up at the Judge's, and took a great interest in Billie. Instead of going back to the school he went to last year, Billie is going on to a school in Virginia, not far from Washington, that Frank suggested sending him to. He is a great believer in the value of environment that is associated with historic traditions."

Kit read this last over twice, but could not agree with it at all. She had always liked the pioneer outlook, the longing to break new trails, the starting of little colonies in clearings of one's own making. If there was an ivy around her castle, she wanted to plant it herself.

"Historic tradition?" repeated Kit. "When all around here are the old Indian trails, and the footprints left by the French explorers. I just wish I could get Billie out here for a little while. He'll settle down in some old school that thinks it is wonderful because John Smith built a campfire on its site once upon a time, or Pocahontas planted corn in its football field."

Kit sighed, tucked her mother's and father's letters in her suit pocket and started off for her favorite lookout point on the bluff. Here, with Sandy crouching at her feet, she read the three letters from Doris, Jean, and Tommy. Jean's was full of plans for going to New York again. Beth, their cousin with whom Jean had stayed the previous winter, had promised her three months at the Art Academy.

"I'm so excited to be going back to New York again. I had a letter from Ralph today and he asked me again if I had decided on an art career. I don't know what to tell him, but I am going to study this winter anyway. Maybe I'll find out this year whether it is worthwhile for me to go on or not. I do know that I love Ralph, but I still have that ambition to do something really important with my life. With the exception of my one trip to New York last year, I have never done anything on my own. Perhaps what I mean is, I want to be independent.

"I shall be coming home weekends this year so I can help Mother and Dad with the rebuilding plans. Besides, I do like living in the country more than the city and it's more for the studying I'm going to do there that I want to go back to New York."

Kit glanced over the rest of the letter hurriedly. Becky had given a neighborhood party and Frank Howard had interested Jean considerably, especially because he told her he was bound for France the first of November. Jean was always so easily impressed just the first few times she met a person. It took Kit a long time to really admit a stranger to her circle of selected ones, although she made friends easily. And she had never quite forgiven Frank Howard for trespassing in the berry patch, even though it had been in the cause of science. Besides, the last year, Jean had seemed to grow aloof from the others. Perhaps it had been her trip away from home or her ambition. Kit could not precisely define the change but it was there, and she felt that Jean troubled herself altogether too much over things unseen.

Doris's letter was all about the opening of school, and Tommy asked questions about Delphi.

"When you write, do tell us about the things that happen there, and just what you think about it. I don't like descriptions in books, I like the talk part. You know what I mean. Jack and I have been helping the carpenters at Woodhow every day after school. The house is coming along fine and the men say we help a lot. Has Uncle Bart got any pets at all?"

Kit laughed over this. If he could only have seen Uncle Bart's pets. His mummy and horned toads, the chimpanzee skull beaming at one from a dark corner, and the Cambodian war mask from another. It seemed as if every time she looked around the house she found something new, and with each curio there went a story. Oddly enough, the Dean thawed more under Kit's persuasion when she begged for the stories than at any other time. After each meal, it was his custom to take a few moments' relaxation in his study. Kit found at these times that he was in his best mood. Relaxed and thoughtful, he would lean back in the deep leather chair between the flat-topped desk and the fireplace, and smoke leisurely. Even his pipe had come from Persia, its amber stem very slender and beautifully curved, its bowl a marvel of carving.

Kit sat pondering over her father's and mother's letters. School would begin in another week, and she was to enter the third year in high school. And yet, after what her father had written, she felt that she was not giving the Dean a square deal.

The odor of tobacco came through the study window, and acting on the spur of the moment, she stepped around the corner of the porch and perched herself on the window sill.

"Are you busy, Uncle Bart?" Anybody who was well-acquainted with Kit would have suspected the gentleness of her tone, but the Dean looked over at her with a little pleased smile. Her coming was almost an answer to his reverie.

"Not at all, my dear, not at all. In fact, I was just thinking of you. I am inclined to think after all that we will begin with the geological periods. I wish you to get your data on pre-historic peoples assembled in your mind before we take up any definite groups."

"That's all right," Kit answered, "I don't mind one bit. I'll do anything you tell me to, Uncle Bart, because," this very earnestly, "I do feel as if I hadn't played quite fair. I mean in coming out here, and landing on you sud-denly, without warning you I was a girl, and I want to make up to you for it in every pos-sible way. I'll study bones and ruins and rocks, and anything you tell me to, but I want to make sure first that you really like me. Just as I am, I mean, before you know for certain whether all this is going to take."

The Dean glanced up in a startled manner and looked at the face framed by the window quite as if he had never really given it an interested scrutiny before. Not being inclined to sentiment by nature, he had regarded Kit so far solely from the experimental standpoint. Since she had turned out to be a girl, he had decided to make the best of it, and at least try the effect of the course of instruction upon her. The personal equation had never entered into his calculation, and yet here was Kit forcing it upon him, quite as plainly as though she had said, "Do you like me or don't you? If you don't, I think I had better go back home."

"Well, bless my heart," he said, rubbing his head. "I thought that we had settled all that. Of course, my dear, the reason I preferred a boy was because, well—" the Dean floundered, "because scientists hold a consensus of opinion that through—hem—through centuries of cultivation, I may say, collegiate development—the male brain offers a better soil, as it were, for the—er—er—"

"The flower of genius?" suggested Kit. "I don't think that's so at all, Uncle Bart, and

I'll tell you why. You take the farm at home. Dad says that our land in Elmhurst is no good because it's been worked over and over, and it's all worn out, but if you plow deep and strike a brand new subsoil you get wonderful crops. Just think what a lovely time you'll have planting crops in my unplowed brain cells."

The first laugh she had ever heard came from the Dean's lips, although it was more of a chuckle. His next question was apparently irrelevant.

"How do you think you're going to like Hope College?"

"All right," Kit responded cheerfully. "I only hope it likes me. I've met a few of the boys and girls through Rex and Aunt Della, and I like them awfully well. At home they're nice to you if they know who you are, and all about your family. But here it seems as if they either like you or not. Just when they first meet you, you're taken right into the fold on the strength of what you are yourself."

The door opened with a little, light, deprecating tap first from Della's fingertips. She glanced around the side of it cautiously to be sure she was not disturbing the Dean, and smiled when she saw the two. The Dean's pipe had gone out, and he was leaning over the desk listening as eagerly as though he had been a boy himself, while Kit, with her hands clasped behind her head and leaning against the window frame, chatted. Usually people conversed with the Dean, they never chatted, and Della realized that Kit had already passed the outposts of the Dean's defenses.

9. Hope College

HOPE COLLEGE was built of gray fieldstone covered with climbing woodbine and Virginia creeper, and it dominated the little town. There were five buildings in the campus group, the main building, laboratory, library and gymnasium, boys' dormitory, and chapel.

Kit never forgot the first morning when the classes met in Assembly Hall, and the Dean addressed them on the work and aims of the coming year. For the life of her, she could not keep her mind on all he was saying or the solemnity of the moment, because just at the very last minute when the chapel chimes stopped ringing, Jeannette Flambeau entered through the heavy doors at the back of the big, crowded hall. It seemed as though everyone's eyes were watching the platform, but Kit saw the slender, silent figure standing there alone. She was dressed in black, a soft wool suit, and her brown hair, no longer in pigtails, hung loosely to her shoulders. She waited there, it seemed to Kit, expectant on the threshold of opportunity, not knowing which way to go, and without a friendly hand extended to her in welcome or guidance.

Georgia Riggs, who sat next to Kit, glanced back to see what had attracted her attention, and made a funny little sound with her mouth.

"I never thought she'd have the nerve to really do it," she whispered. "Isn't she odd?"

A quick impulsive wave of indignation swept over Kit and she rose from her seat, passing straight down the aisle without even being aware of the curious glances which followed her. She took Jeannette by storm.

"You're in my class, aren't you?" she whispered quickly. "It's right over here, and there's a seat beside me. I don't know anyone either, and I'm so glad to see you, so I'll have someone to talk to."

Jeannette never answered, but smiled with a quick flash of appreciation, the smile which always seemed to illumine her grave face. She followed Kit back to her seat, and Georgia exchanged glances with her right-hand neighbor, Amy Parker. Kit was altogether too new to realize just exactly what she had done. Being the Dean's grandniece, she considered herself unconsciously a privileged person. As a matter of course, Della had accompanied her that morning and introduced her to four or five girls in the junior prep class, who came from the representative best families of the town. Also, as a matter of course, she had been welcomed as one of them, but Kit, with her inborn democratic ideas, never even realized that she occupied one of the seats of the mighty, in a circle of the favored few, and that she had smashed all tradition by introducing into that circle a Flambeau. In fact, even if she had known, she would probably have been thoroughly indignant at any such spirit among the girls themselves.

The whole morning was taken up with the assigning of students to classes. Kit loved the curious bustle and excitement of it all. It was so different from the small high school back home, and there were many more boys and girls than she had expected to see. Almost, as she passed from room to room, through the different buildings, she wished she were staying there as a year pupil. Amy introduced her to her closest friend, Peggy Barrows, a girl from South Dakota, who took them up to her quarters in one of the dormitories.

"Gee," Kit said, looking around her, "I wish I were going to live here. Peggy, you'll have to entertain us often. It's so kind of solitary and restful, isn't it, up here?"

"Solitary," scoffed Peggy. "I've been here four days getting settled, and you might just as well call the side show of a circus solitary. There isn't even the ghost of privacy. I'm mobbed every time I try to sit and collect my thoughts.''

''Who wants to collect their thoughts, anyway?'' asked Amy.

''Have you seen Virginia's room? Wait.'' Peggy darted out of her door and across the hall. On the door opposite a card bore the legend in large black letters:

KEEP OUT

STUDY HOUR

''That's absolutely ridiculous,'' she said, tapping just the same. ''Nobody's studying today. Let us in, Ginny.''

A sound of scraping over the floor, and muffled giggles came to waiting ones in the hall, then the door was thrown wide, and Kit caught her first glimpse of Virginia Parks, the most popular girl at Hope. She was about seventeen, but a short, pudgy type, with curly rumpled hair and blue eyes. There were five other girls with her, and papers littered the bed, chairs, and desk.

''We're terribly busy, kids,'' Virginia said, ''What do you want?''

"Just to look at your room. Isn't it pretty, Kit? This is Kit Craig, Ginny."

"Hope you'll like it here," she said. "I'm from the East, too, only not so far as you are, but we think Pennsylvania's east, out here. How do you like the color scheme?"

Kit liked it and said so emphatically. The room was in aqua and coral. The chairs were slipcovered in a coral print on an aqua background and the walls were grey. Kit was invited to sit down on one of the beds.

"I wish I stayed here all the time," Kit exclaimed. "You miss the fun, being a day student, don't you?"

"Never mind," Virginia told her, "we'll have some special celebrations all for you. Now clear out, kids, because I've got a deadline to make."

"Ginny's editor of the *Spirit*," Peg said. "Do you have any journalistic ability, Kit?"

"I've been told I write pretty well, but I never did anything in the newspaper line."

"I think she should have stayed out, she doesn't belong here," one of the other girls was

saying in another part of the room. "None of
that family has ever amounted to anything,
except in the fishing industry—"

But Kit overheard this and interrupted point-
blank. She was sitting up very straight on the
bed, with a certain expression around her
mouth, and a very steady look in her eyes.

"Just a minute," she said quickly. "Do you
mean Jeannette Flambeau? Because if you do,
I don't think that's fair."

Virginia quickly agreed with Kit, but Peg
patted her in a conciliatory manner.

"Now, don't take it to heart so," she said,
"why should it matter to you? Forget it."

But Kit could not be diverted, and the color
rose belligerently in Amy's cheeks, too.

"I don't see why you feel you have to take
Jeannette Flambeau's part," she said. "If you
knew all about her the way we girls do, you'd
let her alone."

"I don't see how she ever came up here anyway," Georgia remarked. "It's just exactly as
if one of her brothers tried to come in. Do you
think the boys would stand for that?"

"Jeepers, why shouldn't they?" demanded Kit hotly. "And I'd like to know what they've got to say about it anyway. I don't think that's the college spirit. Anyone who wants an education and is willing to work for it should be admitted."

"Yes, but if they had any sense at all," responded Georgia placidly, "they wouldn't put themselves into a position of being snubbed. You can talk all you want to about the college spirit from the standpoint of Deans and faculties, but when all's said and done, it's the student spirit that rules. I'll bet that she doesn't stay here a month. She hasn't anyone to help her at home and can't afford tutoring, so she'll just peter out."

The gong sounded in the hall below for afternoon classes, so the discussion came to an abrupt end. Kit found herself watching Jeannette. There was a peculiar aloofness about the girl which seemed to put almost a wall of defense around her. She was intensely interested in everything, one could see that plainly, except the other students, and it seemed as if she simply overlooked them. When Kit came down the stairs, she glanced into the library and saw Jeannette in there alone, bending down before the long wall book shelves. Across the wide hall there were groups of boys and girls in the two long lounges, laughing and talking together, and every couch and chair in both rooms were filled, but Jeannette was alone.

Jeannette was holding a volume of *Treasure Island*, illustrated in color. She turned in surprise at the touch of Kit's hand on her shoulder.

"I thought we could walk down toward the bluff together, because we go the same way," suggested Kit. "How do you like it here?"

"I like it," responded Jeannette slowly, with a certain dignified shyness that was characteristic of her. "My mother has told me all about it. She liked the library when she was here. She told me where her room was upstairs, too, but I didn't want to go up while the girls were there."

"Let's go up now, while they're all downstairs," Kit said impulsively. "I'll take you. Which dorm was she in?"

"Her name was Mary Douglas. It's the Douglas Dormitory. Her father was one of the founders here, Malcolm Douglas."

Kit listened in utter amazement and with a rising sense of joy. Here was Jeannette Flambeau, flouted and disdained by the little crowd of girls who happened to live in a certain district of Delphi, but claiming her grandfather was a founder of the college. At that very moment Kit planned her surprise on the girls.

As they walked through the hall together, Georgia and the others followed them with their glances and smiled. The two paused before a big bronze tablet with the name of the founders on it. There it was, third from the last, Malcolm Douglas.

"He came from Canada," said Jeannette, "and settled here. Later on he went into Minnesota, and on into Dakota. The family was very poor after he died, but my mother came here for two years, and even when I was a little girl, seven or eight years old, before she died, she used to tell me how she loved it, and that I must come here, too."

"Don't any of your brothers want to come? They're all older than you, aren't they."

Jeannette shook her head and smiled curiously. "They are all Flambeau, every one. They eat, and sleep and fish, that's all."

Kit led the way to the upper floor, where the dorms were, and meeting Virginia, she asked the way to the Douglas.

"Why, you were in that one today," answered Virginia in surprise. "It's our dorm, didn't you know?"

"Oh, thanks a lot," Kit said with suspicious alacrity, as she guided Jeannette down the corridor. Virginia glanced back at them both, speculatively, wondering just what special business could take two new day students into the most exclusive dormitory at Hope.

10. The Surprise

KIT deliberately planned her campaign for the following week, and the only girl she took into her confidence was Anne Bellamy. It had been the greatest relief when Anne returned to Delphi for the fall term. There was something good-natured and comfortably serene about Anne that made her companionship a relief from that of the other girls. Jean often said back home that Kit was such a bunch of fireworks herself, she always needed the background of a calm silent night or a placid temperament to set her off properly.

"Golly, Anne," Kit exclaimed, sinking with

a luxurious sigh of content down among the cushions on the broad couch in the Bellamy's living room, "I'd give anything, sometimes, if I'd been an only child. Of course, you've got a brother, but you're the only girl. You don't know what it is to be one of four. I share my room with Doris, back home, and all honors with Jean. Then, of course, there's Tommy, and while we are all crazy about each other, still you do have to elbow your way through a large family, if you want to keep on being yourself. Did you ever read anything of old Joaquin Miller, the poet of the Sierras?"

Anne shook her head.

"No, I don't suppose you have," Kit went on happily. "that's one reason why you and I are going to be terribly good friends, 'cause you don't know everything in creation. It seems to me I can't speak of anything at all at home now that Jean doesn't know more about it than I do, or Doris thinks she does, which is worse. Don't mind me this morning. I just got a family letter, full of don'ts."

"Yes, and you're just as likely as not going to be homesick tomorrow," laughed Anne.

"That isn't what I really came over for. You know Jeannette Flambeau. The kids don't like her going to Hope."

"Don't they?" Anne asked mildly. "Well, what are they going to do about it? I thought that's what colleges were for. Who's against her?"

"I don't think it's exactly anything definite or violent, but you know how awfully uncomfortable they can make her. There's Amy Roberts and Georgia Riggs and Peg Barrows and the Tony Conyers crowd."

"She won't miss anything special, even if they do try to snub her," answered Anne laughingly. "This is my second year at Hope, and I want to tell you right now that Ginny rules in the Douglas dorm. If you can get her on Jeannette's side, the other girls will follow right along like sheep."

"Do you suppose," Kit leaned forward impressively, as she sprang her plan, "do you suppose Ginny would lend her room for a Founders' Tea?"

"A Founders' Tea," repeated Anne. "What's that?"

Kit spoke slowly and with great expression, "A tea in honor of Malcolm Douglas, pioneer founder of Hope College, and grandfather of Jeannette Flambeau."

Anne's blue eyes widened in amazement, and she gasped, "How did you find out? Does Jeannette know?"

"Of course she knows. She told me all about it herself, but I don't think she realizes what a nice handy little club of defense it gives her against the girls. I want to spring it on them at the tea, and you've got to help me get it up. We'll coax Ginny into lending us her room first, and I'll look up all about Malcolm Douglas, and write something clever about the historic founding of Hope. Then we'll send out mysterious little invitations, and just say on them, 'To meet a Founder's granddaughter.' "

"When?" asked Anne reflectively. "You ought to do it soon, so if it works they'll take her into the different clubs right away. I think you ought to try to see Virginia today after classes and get her advice. Another thing, Kit, do you suppose Jeannette would have any things of her grandfather's we could kind of spring on them unexpectedly?"

Kit's eyes kindled with appreciation. "That's a worthy thought. Sort of corroborative evidence, as it were. Anne, you're a genius." She jumped up from the couch and started to leave. "I think it's up to me to go and prepare Virginia. You make out a list of things that we'll want for the tea. You'd better be the refreshment chairman, and we'll try and make it a week from next Saturday."

"Too far off," Anne warned. "Better do it while it's fresh in your mind, before you start lectures."

"I guess I'll go over now. It's only a little after five, and that'll keep me from answering the family letters until I've calmed down. If you see anyone looking for me, tell them I'll be right back. I'll stop in the library and look up Malcolm's historic record, on my way, so you may truthfully announce I'm doing research."

Kit went up the hill road buoyantly. She liked to set a goal for herself this way. Delphi had appeared rather barren as a field for her real endeavor, but now with the opening of school, she could see her way ahead to starting something, which she sincerely hoped she could finish. Coming along the sidewalk that bounded the campus on the south, she met Ginny on her way back from the post office

"This is ever so-much better than going upstairs," Kit said. "Let's walk around the campus twice, while I unburden my soul."

At the second lap, the whole plan had been matured by Virginia's quick sympathy and understanding

"And it will do them good, too," she said as they parted. "That's not the college spirit by a long shot, and you're perfectly right, Kit,

but just the same it's easier to get it across to
the girls in this way with a nice friendly ac-
companiment of sandwiches, and iced tea. And
whatever you do, don't breathe a single word
to anybody. I wouldn't even tell Jeannette
herself that she is to be the guest of honor.
She'd run like a deer, if she even suspected it.''

The date of the Founders' Tea was set for
the following Saturday. Kit composed the invitations herself and wrote them on small
cards.

Saturday, October Second, Three to Five.
You are invited to attend a Founders' Tea,
Douglas Dormitory, Hope College,
Virginia Parks' Study.

"Diffident, modest, and correct," said Kit,
critically, when she showed them to Anne.
"Now, what are you going to have to eat,
Anne? Isn't there something besides just plain
tea? Couldn't we fix up some kind of glorified
lemonade?"

"I've got it all down," answered Anne.

"Grape juice, ginger ale and lemons. Sound good? And six kinds of sandwiches and cookies."

"It's perfectly swell," exclaimed Kit. "Aunt Della told me when I first started in that I could give a party for the girls, and this is it. After it is all over I'll tell her about Jeannette, and I know she'll enjoy it and approve."

"Is Ginny going to decorate the study for the occasion?" asked Anne. "We ought to have something sort of different, don't you think?"

"Pioneer stuff would be the only thing, and I don't know where we'd scare that up."

"There's a whole cabinet of them in the Dean's room at the college."

The two girls looked at each other wisely. The subject really needed no argument or discussion. Kit said briefly, "I'll try. I think I can get some of them anyway if I approach Uncle Bart as a humble student seeking knowledge."

All unprepared for the onslaught, the Dean sat enjoying his after-dinner smoke that evening when Kit came to the door and knocked.

"Come in," he called a little bit testily, looking over his glasses at the intruder. "I don't think I can talk with you just now, my dear," he said, "I'm very busy working out a dynasty problem."

"Oh, but I'd love to help," Kit pleaded, "and I did help before on the aborigines of Japan, didn't I? I even remember their names, the Ainos."

"This is early Egyptian. Something you know nothing whatever about."

"Just mummies?" inquired Kit.

The Dean coughed, and turned back to the pamphlets before him. "Remains have been discovered," he began in quite the tone he used in Assembly, "of the lost tribe of the Nemi. When the Greeks, my dear, obtained a foothold in Carthage and along the Mediterranean coast, the Nemi remained unconquered and retreated to the mountain fastnesses, west of the source of the Nile."

"Well, I know all about that," Kit answered, perching herself on the arm of a chair, across from him. "Just see," and she counted off on her fingers, "Livingstone-Stanley—Victoria Falls—Zambesi—and Kipling wrote all about the people in *Fuzzy-Wuzzy*."

"No, no, no, not a bit like it." the Dean exclaimed. "My dear child, learn to think in centuries and epochs. The long and short of it is, there have been some very wonderful remains of the Nemi recently discovered, and I have been honored by a commission from the Institute to write a complete summary of the results of the expedition and its historic significance."

"Don't you wish you'd been there when they dug them up? That's what I'd love, the exploring part. I should think it would be dreadfully dry trying to make bones sit up and talk, when you are so far away from it all."

"They are not sending me bones," replied the Dean with dignity, "but they are sending me the Amenotaph urn, and a sitting image of Annui. I believe with these two I shall be able to establish as a fact the survival of the Greek influence in ancient Egypt. My dear, you have no idea," he added warmly, "how much this explains if it is true. There may be even Phoenician data before I finish investigating."

"Phoenicians," thought Kit, although she said nothing. "Yes, I do remember about them, too. Tin—ancient Britain—and something about Carthage." Then she said aloud very positively and earnestly, "I know I can help you a lot with this, Uncle Bart, if you will only let me, because history is my favorite subject, and the reason I came to speak to you tonight is this. We girls are going to have a Founders' Tea, Saturday afternoon. Just a little informal affair, but I'd like to give it a—" She hesitated for the right word, and the Dean nodded encouragingly, being in a better mood.

"Semblance of verity? Are you preparing a treatise?"

"No. I want something they can look at. And I knew if I told you about it, you'd let us take a few of the old things out of that cabinet in your room at the college. All I need would be—well, say a few portraits of any of the founders of Hope, and any of the relics of the Indians or French explorers.''

The Dean graciously detached a key from the ring at one end of his watch chain.

Kit left with it as though she bore a trophy. The next day the last preparations were completed for impressing on the girls of Hope College the honor of having a Founder's granddaughter in their midst.

11. The Mysterious Guest

"I THINK you ought to preside, Kit," Virginia said as she arranged the table. "It's your party, and you ought to serve."

"Takes too much concentration," Kit returned. "Anne'll help you. I want to have my mind perfectly clear to manage the thing. You see, Jeannette doesn't know a thing about it yet, and there's no knowing how she'll take it. Wouldn't it be funny if she got proud and haughty and marched away from our Founders' Tea?"

"I don't think you ought to spring it until after we've had refreshments. Food has such a mellowing effect on people. It's all a question of tact, though. If I were you, I'd talk to them in an intimate sort of way instead of lingering too much on the historic value. Better straighten Malcolm, over there. He looks kind of topply."

Kit regarded the framed steel engraving of Malcolm Douglas almost fondly. It occupied a prominent spot specially cleared for it in the middle of the wall.

Backed by Della's approval and interest, Kit had called at several homes where the descendants of other founders lived, and the results were gratifying. Mrs. Peter Bradbury had contributed two Indian blankets and a hunting bag, besides an old pair of saddle bags used by an early missionary bishop in the Northwest. From the cabinet in the Dean's room had come mostly records, old documents carefully framed, and several letters written by the founders themselves.

"Golly," Kit said as she gave a last touch to her exhibit, "of course these are important, but I like the Indian and hunting things best. I wish I could run away with that double pair of buffalo horns that belonged to Dr. Gleason's granduncle or somebody. I like them better than anything."

A quick rap came on the door, and before Virginia could even call "come in" Peggy entered with her usual galaxy behind her, Amy, Georgia, and a newcomer from Iowa, Henrietta Jenkins.

"Tony Conyers sent word she'd be ready in five minutes," said Georgia. "She's got a lot of the girls in there with her. Ginny, I think this is a perfectly stupendous idea of yours."

"'Tisn't mine," answered Virginia, "it's Kit's. This is her party. Her coming-out party at Hope."

"Oh, are you the founder's granddaughter?" Amy inquired, her eyes opening wide.

"No, I'm not," replied Kit. "I wish this minute I could tell you about my ancestors. I've got some beauts. Peggy, don't sit on the almonds. They're right behind you in that glass dish."

The room filled up rapidly with people. Kit declared after she had been the rounds four times that she felt exactly like the lecturer in a museum, telling the history of the relics over and over again. Nobody but Anne knew how anxious she was as the minutes slipped by and no Jeannette appeared. It would never do to have a climax happen without the surprise of her presence to carry it off. The refreshments had all been served, and the clock on top of the bookshelves showed that it was five, when Virginia called; "You'd better start in on your Founders' talk, Kit. We've only got about half an hour."

There was a baffled look in Kit's eyes, as she picked up the challenge and rose from her chair. Virginia must know perfectly well how untimely it was to start to spring the surprise while there was a running chance of Jeannette appearing. Still there was a hush, and the girls faced her expectantly.

"As you all know," began Kit, "the old bronze tablet in the lower hall carries names on its roll of honor which not only uphold the glory of Hope College, but also of the entire town of Delphi, of the entire state, I may say of Wisconsin.

"There are few of us here today, if any," continued Kit slowly, one eye watching the concrete walk across the campus from the nearest window, "who can boast of a Hope founder in her family."

"I can, almost," interrupted Tony, "my sister Marie was engaged for a little while to Bernard Giron. If she had only married him, we would have had a 'Founder' in the family."

"Tony," said Kit, severely, "I am dealing with facts, not prospects, and you ought not reveal any family secrets, either. I say it is a great honor to be a direct descendant of a 'Founder,' and we have one in our class. A girl, too modest to take advantage of her grandfather's record." She paused impressively, but with a quickening gleam in her eyes, as there suddenly came in view a hurrying figure in a gray suit on the campus walk. It was

Jeannette herself, late, but in time to create the desired sensation.

Kit drew a deep breath, and plunged back to her subject, considering exactly the time it would take for the belated guest to reach the study.

"Since all the girls here belong to this dormitory, it seems appropriate that the founder whose memory we honor should be Malcolm Douglas. His portrait hangs on the wall, evidently taken from an old likeness." Oh, how she wished the family could hear her now! "There is no more adventurous or thrilling career in the annals of historic Delphi than that of the illustrious Scotchman. Making his way through the perils of the wilderness, he came from Quebec with a party of fur traders and pioneer explorers."

"Don't hit too far back, Kit," interrupted Peggy, alertly. "If he was a founder, you can't have him trotting over wilderness trails with Marquette and Lasalle, you know."

"Nevertheless," responded Kit, ignoring

her, "he is one of the founders of this college. He came here in his early twenties, and married Lucia, the daughter of Captain Peter Morton. Their daughter was Mary, and, girls, she was the mother of one of our classmates, the very same Mary who went through Hope and graduated with high honors. You'll find her initials carved in Number 10 across the hall, and her portrait—the only one I could find—is in this graduating group."

The girls all crowded forward to look at the group photograph which Kit held out to them, just as a knock came at the door. For one dramatic instant Kit held the knob, her back against the door as she announced in almost a whisper, "The granddaughter of Malcolm Douglas."

The girls leaned forward, eagerly, every eye fixed upon the door. As Kit said later to Anne, "Goodness knows who they expected to see, but I almost felt as though I had promised them a two-headed man, and then had sprung Jeannette. Wasn't she marvelous, Anne? The way she stood the introduction and the shock of finding herself the guest of honor. As I looked at her, I thought to myself, you may be Douglas, and you may be Morton, fine old Scotch and English stock, but if it wasn't for the dash of debonair Flambeau in you too, you could never carry this off the way you're doing."

Jeannette was not the only person present who had to fall back on inherent caste for their manners of the moment, but Tony was the only one that gave an audible gasp. Even Peggy and Georgia smiled, and greeted the Founder's granddaughter in the proper spirit.

She was dressed in a plain gray suit, but Kit gloried in the way she took her place beside Virginia at the table, and answered the questions of the girls with laughing ease.

"Of course," she said, with the little slight accent she seemed to have caught from her father and old Grandmother Flambeau, "I thought everyone in Delphi knew. For myself,

I am proud of him, and of all my mother's people, but I am also proud of being a Flambeau. You girls do not know perhaps that some of my father's people helped to found Fort Dearborn, and they were very brave and courageous voyagers in the early days of New France."

Peggy really rose to the occasion remarkably, Kit thought. Probably the most jealously guarded membership in the prep classes was that of the Portia Club, and yet, before the tea was over, she had invited Jeannette to attend the next meeting and be proposed for membership.

"We're not going to try a whole play at first, just famous scenes, and I know you'd fit in somewhere and enjoy it. Don't you want to, Jeannette?"

Jeannette shrugged her shoulders, and said, "I shall be glad to help always, if you wish to make me one of you."

"What do you think of that?" Anne said on

the way home. "Kit, you certainly have discovered a flower that was born to blush unseen."

"It will take her out of her shell, anyway," Kit replied happily. "And I do think the girls came up to the mark splendidly. How I'd like to hear what they're saying about us now, behind our backs, but they acted their parts nobly when I swung that door open, and there stood, just Jeannette!"

12. Homesick

No QUALMS of homesickness visited Kit the first two months after school opened. Not even New England could eclipse the glory of autumn when it swept in full splendor over this corner of the Lake States. Down east there was a sort of middle-aged relaxation to this season of the year.

But here autumn came as a gypsy. The stretches of forest that fringed the ravines rioted in color. The lakes seemed to take on the very deepest sapphire blue. No hush lay over the land as it did in the East, but there were wild sudden storm flurries, a feeling in the air as if there might be a regular tornado any minute.

Hardly a Saturday passed but what Kit was included in some fall picnic hike or else she was off to a football game. The Dean never joined these, but occasionally Della did and thoroughly enjoyed them. And once, toward the end of November, in the very last of Indian summer weather, they took a weekend tour up to Eau Claire and Chippewa Falls.

"I only wish," Rex said, "that we could come up here next spring when they have their big logging time. It's one of the greatest sights you ever saw, Kit. I have seen the logs jammed out there in the river until they looked like a giant's game of jackstraws. Maybe we could arrange a trip, don't you think so, Mom?"

"I don't see any reason why not," replied Mrs. Bellamy.

"But I won't be here then," protested Kit.

"Oh, you'll stay till the end of the spring term, dear," Della corrected, and right then Kit experienced her first pang of homesickness.

Would she really be away from home until next June? Even with this novelty of recreation, backed by wealth, she felt suddenly as though she could have slipped away from it all without a single regret, just to find herself safely back home with the family.

One weekend while Jean was home at Maple Grove, she and her mother were talking together about Jean's work. Doris and Tommy with Jack had walked over to Woodhow to help Mr. Craig, so Jean and her mother were alone.

Each time Jean came home she found herself turning with a sigh of relief and safety from the city life to the peace of the hills. It was her comment on this to her mother that had prompted their talk.

"Are you going to begin looking into job possibilities while you are in New York, Jean?" asked her mother. "I think if you are really serious about a career, you should begin getting interviews for a job next year."

"No Mom," replied Jean. "I think I have

reached an important decision. I wasn't going to tell you until my course was over and I was positive I was right, but I'll tell you now since you asked. I love Ralph more than I do a career and if he asks me to marry him, I'll say yes. I've learned to analyze my feelings and I am quite sure my love for art is only a hobby. To have a happy marriage like yours and Dad's is, is the most important thing I want."

"You have made a wise and difficult decision, my dear," said Mrs. Craig tenderly. "Your father and I have felt all along that Ralph was ideally suited for you, but we wanted you to make your own decisions first."

Just then, the mailman brought Kit's next letter and Jean read it over her mother's shoulder. A little puzzled frown drew Jean's straight dark brows together.

"She's getting homesick, Mother. Kit never writes tenderly like that unless she feels a heart throb. I never thought she'd last as long as she has—"

But Mrs. Craig looked dubious.

"She seems to have made such a good impression. I hate to have her spoil it by jumping back too soon. It's such an opportunity for her."

Jean stopped washing the dishes and gazed out of the kitchen window toward the fields, where none but the crows could find a living now.

"I don't blame her a bit if she wants to come back home before summer, Mom. Money isn't everything."

"That's true," sighed her mother. "But it's a shame not to take advantage of it when it comes your way."

"Just the same, if I were you, I'd write and tell Kit that she could come home at the Christmas vacation if she wanted to."

But Becky took an entirely different view of the matter when she was consulted. "Fiddlesticks," she said. "No girl of Kit's age knows what she wants two minutes of the time. She isn't needed here at all, Margaret. Doris is getting plenty old enough to take hold and help."

So two letters went back to Kit, and in hers Mrs. Craig could not resist slipping a hint that perhaps it would be a wise thing to ask the Dean about ending her visit at Christmas time.

But Jean added in hers, "Mother's afraid you are homesick, or that they may be tired of you by this time, but if I were in your place, I'd try to stay until June. Dad thinks the house may be done in time for us to go into it next month, but we've had lots of wet weather, and Becky says it would be horribly unhealthful to move in before the plaster has had a chance to thoroughly dry. Matt goes down every day with Dad, and they've kept the fire going in the furnace, so I suppose that will help some, but there isn't a particle of need for your coming back, except Mother's dread that you may be homesick, and you're getting too old to mollycoddle yourself, where there's a big interest at stake."

Kit read this with a frown. "It's so nice to have been born Jean, and speak on any subject as the oldest," she said scornfully. "I know perfectly well that Mom needs me when she is moving back into the new house, and I never expected to stay so long when I came, anyway."

She stopped short, meditating on just what this queer, choky feeling was that had swept over her. She knew that she would have given up everything, the new friends she had made, and all the winter's fun at Hope College, just to be safely back home.

13. Frank Apologizes

Kɪᴛ was doing some homework in the library one Saturday morning, when all at once she was conscious of someone who stood at the west end of the room, looking at her. For a moment Kit was absolutely speechless, not believing the evidence of her own eyes. But the next minute Billie's own laugh, when he found out he had been discovered, startled her with its reality.

"Billie Ellis," she exclaimed, springing to her feet and scattering reference books and notepaper helter-skelter. "How on earth did you ever get way out here?"

Billie colored slightly, as he always did at

any display of emotion, and tried to act as if
it were the most natural and ordinary thing in
the world for him to appear at Delphi, when
he was supposed to be in Washington in
school.

"We had our exams last week, and Frank
had to come out to Minnesota for the government, so he took me along to help him."

"Billie, are you really after bugs and things
—I mean, are you going to really be a naturalist?"

"I guess you'd kind of call it being a business naturalist," laughed Billie. "I don't
think I'll ever live in a shack on a mountain-
side, and write beautiful things about them,
now that I know Frank. You want to roll up
your sleeves and pitch in like he does."

"Is he here now?" asked Kit eagerly.

"Yep." Billie nodded out of the window
toward Kemp Hall, the boys' dormitory.
"After we found out that you didn't live here,
we were going on down to the Dean's to find
you, but he looked over the boys' freshman

class, and found he had a cousin or nephew or somebody on the list, Clayton Diggs."

"I know him," Kit said. "He's awfully nice. I've got to be back for lunch, and you're coming down with me, of course. How long can you stay?"

"Just this afternoon. We're going back on the five forty-five, and catch the night express out of Chicago. If you wait here, I'll chase after Frank, 'cause he'll want to have lunch with the Diggs boy, and he can join us later."

Kit walked along the path which crossed the campus. The coming of Billie unexpectedly, just at a time when she was feeling her first homesickness, struck Kit as a rare piece of luck. But with only five hours to visit with him, she knew it would be all the harder after he had gone. He joined her on a run as she reached the sidewalk, and they hurried down to the Dean's just in time for lunch. Kit beamed when she introduced her friend from the hills to Della and the Dean.

"Don't you remember, Uncle Bart," she asked eagerly, "my talking about Billie? Well, here he is."

The Dean's gray eyes twinkled as he surveyed Billie over the tops of his glasses. "You come highly recommended, young man," he said.

"You could have a lovely time studying over Uncle Bart's Egyptian scarabs, Bill," said Kit. "Weren't you telling me something about a place in China where they had a whole grove filled with sacred silkworms, Aunt Della? You see, Billie's main interest is insects and birds."

Miss Peabody smiled and nodded, looking from one young face to the other. Never before had youngsters sat lunching at that table with her and her brother in quite such a way. The Dean usually took his meals in absolute silence when they were alone together, for he held that desultory conversation disturbed his train of thought. But since Kit's coming, it had been impossible to check her flow of talk, until now the Dean actually missed it if she happened not to be there.

After lunch they all went into the library to look over the Dean's newly arrived treasures, the Amenotaph urn and the statue of Annui.

"Well, gol-lee," exclaimed Kit, as she stood before the plain, squat, terra-cotta urn, "is that the royal urn? I expected to see something enormous, like everything else that is wonderful and ancient in Egypt. '

"My dear," the Dean replied happily as he bent down to trace the curious, cuneiform markings that circled the urn. "This antedates the time of the Captivity and Moses. I cannot tell positively, until I have opened it and deciphered what I can of the papyrus rolls within. If it should go back to Moses, it will be wonderful. I cannot believe that it is contemporary with Nineveh. Della, you can recall how overjoyed I was when we unearthed that library of precious clay under the Nineveh mounds years ago. Think of reading something which was written by living man several thousand years before that."

"What fun it must have been," Billie remarked. "If you wanted to write anything in those days, you just picked up a handful of mud and made a little brick out of it, and wrote away with a stick, didn't you?"

"Stylus, my boy, stylus," corrected the Dean absently. "Yes, it did away with much of our modern detail."

"Where's the statue, Uncle Bart?" Kit asked.

"It's just behind you, my dear. And it's perfect. Perfect." murmured the Dean.

Kit turned, expecting to face one of the usual blandly smiling Egyptian pieces of art, with a few wings scattered over it here and there. But instead, there stood in the center of the table a strangely attenuated figure about three feet high. It had a head that was a cross between an intelligent antelope and a rather toplofty baby rat. Its arms were extended at sharp angles, and seemed to be pointing in arch accusation at someone. Wings spread fanwise from the shoulders, and its feet were like those of a griffin.

"I never thought it would look just like that, did you, Billie?" Kit asked confidentially, when they started back to the campus later.

"Well, I knew what to expect, because we've been going to the Smithsonian Institute pretty often," replied Billie. "Some of them look worse than that. But they can't beat our own Alaskan and Mexican ones. I wonder what people were thinking about back in those days to worship that sort of thing?"

But Kit caught sight of five of the girls just rounding the corner and she waved to them to come over, much to Billie's inward disgust. While he thoroughly approved of Kit, he viewed the average girl with indifference. But Kit introduced him in a casual manner which put him at his ease, and when they started up the path, it was Tony Conyer who had taken possession of Billie, and was interesting him by telling of her father's big stock farm in northern Wisconsin.

They found Frank Howard waiting for them outside the boys' dorm and Clayton was with him. The girls got Kit aside and Amy faced her accusingly.

"You never told us a word about this boy," she declared, "and all the time you've had him up your sleeve. Explain please."

Kit laughed at them and said, "Well, he's a relative, if you must know. He's my father's first cousin's husband's grandson. Now what are you going to do about it?"

Rather mollified, the girls rejoined the boys on the steps in front of the dorm. "I suppose Hope looks pretty small to you after the universities back East," Georgia said to Billie.

"Looks swell to me," returned Billie. "I think you can have lots more fun in a place like this than you can at the big schools. But don't get the idea I'm going to college now, I'm just at prep school and taking up a few extra courses outside with Frank."

"What kind of courses?" asked Georgia.

"Science and physics, but specially ento-
mology and forestry. He's in government
service. I wish I knew all he does. It's wonderful to have a friend like Frank."

Kit was behind the others with Amy and
Anne. Now that they had joined the others,
and the girls were talking about Frank also,
she had become strangely silent.

"You don't know him very well, do you?"
Amy asked. "I mean, he isn't related to you."

Kit shook her head with bland indifference.

"He's a friend of Billie's. I only met him at
home when he came to chase a gypsy moth in
Elmhurst."

She did not add that with Tommy's help
and able cooperation, she had managed to
curtail the chase of the gypsy moth, tem-
porarily, by holding the chaser captive in the
family corncrib, but she inwardly suspected
that Frank was remembering it. Every once in
a while she caught him looking at her, with a

look of amused retrospection that made her
vaguely uncomfortable.

As they left the campus, Georgia, leading
with Billie, took the street that led to the
bluffs overlooking the lake, and somehow or
other in the scramble down the narrow path-
ways, Kit found Frank at her elbow. No one
could have been more dignified or distant in
her manner than Kit, but Frank refused to be
frozen out.

"I've just found out something, Kit," he
said genially. "I forgave you long ago for
locking me up in your corncrib and nearly
landing me in the local jail, but you don't
forgive me one bit for trespassing in your
berry patch."

Kit's profile tilted ever so slightly upward.
She had thoroughly made up her mind that
very day when Mr. Hicks made his memorable
and fruitless journey to Woodhow that not
even government experts had any right to
climb over fences into people's private property without first asking permission. Perhaps

the sudden popularity of the trespasser with all the rest of the family had something to do with Kit's stand against him. Even Doris had remarked that she didn't see how Kit could ever have imagined that a person looking like Frank could be a berry thief.

"I don't want you to forgive me," she said calmly. "I've never been one bit sorry for it. I think you ought to have come up to the house and asked permission to go in there. And you never said that you were sorry. It always seemed to me as if you rather acted as if you thought it was a good joke"—she hesitated a moment, before adding pointedly— "on me."

"Suppose I apologize now." Frank's tone was absolutely serious, but Kit, with one quick look at the precipitous path ahead of them, laughed.

"Not here, please. Wait until we hit the level shore. You do really have to pay attention on this path, or you miss your footing and toboggan all at once."

"Then, suppose," he persisted. "we just consider that I have apologized. And if you accept, you can raise your right hand at me."

Kit immediately raised her left one. Before he could say any more, she had hurried ahead and caught up with the rest.

14. The Secret in the Urn

It was not until after they had gone, when Kit was by herself, that she remembered all Billie had told her at the very last of his stay.

They had walked along the lake shore together, a little behind the others, after they had visited the Flambeau family.

"You haven't told me anything at all," Kit said, "about home. When were you in Elmhurst last?"

"Just before we came here," Billie answered.

"Was everything all right?" Billie hesitated. "Oh, for heaven's sake, Billie, tell me if there is anything. You can't give me any nervous shocks at all, and I'm dying to find an excuse to get back home."

"Why, there isn't anything the matter, exactly," Billie said cheerfully, but with a reservation in his tone that made Kit impatient. "The only thing that I know about, I heard Grandfather telling Uncle Tom. I don't suppose I ought to repeat it either."

"Honestly, Billie, you make me so exasperated at times. How dare you keep back any news of my family from me?"

"It was something about losing some stocks or dividends or something like that. I guess it hit Grandfather, too, but I heard him say that there wasn't a farm up there that couldn't support itself, properly run, and he guessed they'd all weather the storm."

Billie was inclined to take an optimistic view of the whole affair. "Grandfather said that there was no cause for worry," he went on. "It was just a case of pitch in and get your living out of the farms again."

"Yes," said Kit with scorn, "get your living out of the farms. That's all very well for him to say, when he's got everything to do with, and twenty of the best cows in the county, but we moved up there on hope and a shoestring. And we've never really raised anything except children and chickens."

"Frank says your place, if it was properly worked, would make one of the finest fruit farms up there, 'cause your land all slopes to the south as far as the river. He says if he had it he'd sell off the heavy timber for cash and put the money right into hardy varieties of fruit and hogs."

Kit laughed. "Can't you see Doris' face over the hogs, with all her aristocratic ideas? Did he tell Dad that?"

"I don't know," Billie said doubtfully. "Uncle Tom's kind of hard to get confidential with over his own affairs, but I wouldn't worry, Kit, if I were you. Things always come out all right."

"They do not," returned Kit calmly. "Even so, thanks ever so much for telling me, Billie. You may have changed the course of destiny, because I can tell you now I'm going home."

After dinner that night Kit was out for a walk alone with only Sandy for company. Kit was wondering whether it would be best to write first to her mother or to Jean. Jean would be in New York anyway, so perhaps she wouldn't know any more about it than Kit did. How she wished to know just exactly what the family's plans were for the winter.

Finally she decided to write to Becky. Even though her decision might not be a favorable one, you always felt sure you were getting it straight without any affectionate bias.

Accordingly, a confidential appeal went East, and back came the reply by return mail, as Kit had known it would.

Dear Kit,

    I had been thinking about you when your letter came, so I suppose our thoughts must have crossed.

    There's no doubt at all but what your mother needs you badly right here, especially with Jean in New York. What Billie told you was about the truth.

If I were you, I'd have a heart-to-heart talk with the Dean himself, and I know your mother will be just as relieved as can be to hear you're homeward bound.

Lovingly,
Becky.

Kit was delighted over the letter, and went directly to the Dean with its message. He was deeply engrossed in getting up his first notes and commentaries on the urn and statue. It had not seemed for the past two or three weeks as if he resided any longer in Delphi at all. Kit told Della she was positive he was wandering through Egypt all the time, the Egypt of five thousand years ago. And it was only the shadow of his self that seemed to sit closeted for hours in the study.

He hardly glanced up now as she came in, but smiled and nodded when he saw who it was, keeping on with his writing.

"Just hand me that volume on the second shelf to your right by the door. Second volume,

Explorations in Upper Egypt, look up Seti the First in the index."

Kit found the place and laid it before him, perching herself on one end of the desk, as she always did when she wanted to attract his attention. The little statuette of Annui smiled grotesquely down upon her from its pedestal. The urn stood in a handy place of honor upon the desk itself as the Dean had been deciphering the inscriptions upon it.

"I hate to disturb you, Uncle Bart," Kit began, with the directness so characteristic of her, "but I really think I ought to go back home. You've been wonderful to give me such a long visit, and I've enjoyed the school work immensely, but somehow I begin to feel like a soldier who has been away on a furlough. It's time for me to get back, because Mother needs me."

The Dean glanced up in surprise, and came slowly out of his dream of concentration as the meaning of her words dawned upon him.

"Why, my dear child," he exclaimed, "this is very sudden. There has never been any question about your going back, at least—" He coughed. "Not since we became acquainted with you. Has anything happened?"

"Why, nothing special—I mean, nothing tragic. It's only this, Dad's lost a lot of money all at once. He did have a little income, enough so we never have had to depend on the farm entirely, but now, even that has been swept away."

"Tom never had any head for business." The Dean tapped one hand lightly with his glasses in an absent-minded musing way that nearly drove Kit frantic. "But what can you do about it, my dear? Surely by returning at such a time you merely add to your father's burdens."

"No, I won't," Kit answered. "Because I've got a plan that I've been thinking about for ever and ever so long. I'm going to try and persuade Dad to let us put in hogs."

"Hogs," repeated the Dean in a baffled tone.

"Hogs, my dear. Who ever heard of raising hogs when they could raise anything else at all?"

"Well, we're going to if Dad will let me. I just can't stay here in this beautiful place with nothing to worry over, while the family are all worried to death."

There was silence in the old study. The Dean was looking straight at Annui as if for inspiration. He had laid out his own career himself, and had carried every ambition to completion and reality. The last twenty years had been years of fruition, of honors freely given, years of fulfillment. He had not been, like Judge Ellis, intolerant of other men's failures; he had simply ignored them, never feeling any responsibility toward the weaker ones who fell in the race. In his way, he prided himself on a gentle, aloof philosophy of life which left him the boundaries of the study as a horizon of happiness.

Probably not until that moment had he realized the gradual revolutionary process Kit had been putting him through ever since her arrival. She had trained him into having an interest in other people and things, until now it was impossible for him not to see the picture of Woodhow as she did. He resolved to help Tom Craig out as well.

"How did you find out about this, my dear?" he asked.

"Well," Kit replied, honestly "partly from Billie and partly from a letter from Becky. You know Becky, don't you, Uncle Bart?"

The Dean's eyes twinkled reminiscently. "Oh, yes, I remember Rebecca well. She used to bully me outrageously. But you're perfectly right, my dear. I can quite see why you feel that you are needed. You had better start for home as soon as you can."

The next thing was to break the news gently and convincingly to the family. Kit figured it out from all sides, and finally decided to walk right up to the horns of the dilemma in a fearless attack. Writing back a long, newsy letter to her mother, she simply tacked on the postscript, "Don't be at all surprised to see me arrive around Christmas."

The girls took her coming departure with many objections, but Kit was not to be persuaded to stay. The Saturday before she left the many friends she had made came over in the afternoon to say goodbye. Late in the day, Kit saw Jeannette Flambeau coming up the drive.

"It was awfully nice of you to come, Jeannette," she exclaimed. "I've been watching for you."

"I tried to come earlier, but I couldn't," smiled Jeannette. "Will you write to me when you are away?"

"I'd love to. You know it's a queer thing, Jeannette, but really and truly, out of all the girls I have met here I feel better acquainted with you than with any of them."

Kit said this rather slowly, as if it were a sort of self-revelation which she had just discovered that minute. And yet it was true. She had enjoyed the class friendships at Hope im-

mensely, but Jeannette had seemed to stand out
from the rest of the girls as a distinctly interesting personality.

Jeannette smiled at Kit's remark.

"I have heard my grandmother say that in
her girlhood her people of the northern forests
pledged their friendships by saying, 'While the
grass grows and the waters run, so long shall
we be friends.'" She turned and smiled at Kit
her grave-eyed slow smile. "I will say that to
you now, before you go."

Kit laid one arm around her shoulders. "Me
too," she answered, "sounds like the blood-
brother vow they used to take."

The next evening Kit was to leave Delphi.
She found it hard to say goodbye to her aunt
and uncle.

"We shall miss you, Kit," said Della, "but
if it gives you any pleasure, my dear, I want to
tell you it was your coming which opened my
eyes to the folly of sitting with empty hands
while there was work to be done. I don't

think I can ever belong to the rocking-chair squad again, without a guilty conscience."

Kit hugged her fervently. "Oh, but you're a dear, Aunt Della, to say such things. I only wish I could stay right here and be in two places at once. I'll tell you what I've learned here, organization." Kit said this very firmly and earnestly. "Back home they say I know just what I want to do, but I don't know how to do it. Now, I know what I want to do. I want to go back home and organize."

"The Dean wanted to have a little talk with you before dinner, dear. I think you'd better go in now, because we want to reach the station in plenty of time. Don't talk too long. You know how he is when he gets absorbed in anything."

Kit promised and joined the Dean. He had carried back the statue of Annui and stood before it regarding it with perplexity. Kit slipped her arm through his. It seemed as though there had sprung up a new comradeship and understanding between them since their last talk.

"Won't he tell you his secrets, Uncle Bart?" she asked. "He has such an aggravating smile, just as if he were amused at baffling you."

"I am baffled," the Dean conceded genially. "I've reached a certain point and there is a blank which no historic record seems to fill. I thought when I had restored the inscription on the urn that it would tell me several of the missing points, but it seems to be merely a sort of sacred invocation. I am amazed at the urn being hollow. Every other memorial urn which I found during our excavations in Egypt was sealed, and upon being opened we always found rolls of papyrus within. I am disappointed."

Kit lifted the urn very carefully and stared at it, reflectively. "What does the inscription say?" Kit asked.

"It merely traces the origin of King Ameno-taph to the god Thoth," said the Dean, thoughtfully, "that is, the Egyptian Hermes, or Mercury, as we know him, and it is extremely vague, being a curious mixture of the Coptic and the ancient Aramaic."

"But what does it say?" asked Kit again.

The Dean followed the curious markings on the urn with his fingertip, bending forward as he did so. "It says, 'Amenotaph, born of Thoth, shall reign in wisdom. Kings shall serve at his foot stool. Ra shall shine upon him. He shall lie in peace, encompassed by Ra.'"

"Is that all?"

"That is all," sighed the Dean. "It seems merely a laudatory sentiment."

"Who was Ra?" asked Kit curiously, running her hand around the top of the urn.

"The Sun god. His symbol was the circle. You see it here."

Kit repeated again slowly, what her uncle had just read. Then she shook the urn close to her ear.

"My dear child, do be careful," cried the Dean, "it's priceless."

But Kit put it under one arm as though it

had been a milk pail and tapped around the inside with her knuckles, listening.

"That's a perfectly good hollow jug," she said solemnly. "Just you tap it, and listen, Uncle Bart. I'll bet they've hidden something inside the outside and that Ra has guarded it all these years."

"Just a moment, just a moment, my dear," exclaimed the Dean, smiling like a happy boy. "You've given me an idea. This may be a cryptogram, or an ideographic cipher. Just a moment, now, don't speak to me."

He sat down at the desk and figured laboriously for nearly twenty minutes, working out the inscription in cipher, while Kit stared at him delightedly. After all, it was gratifying, she thought, to have somebody in the family who could take a little remark made thousands of years ago in Egypt and make sense out of it today. She waited patiently until he had finished. His hands were trembling as he reached for the urn.

"The circle," he repeated, "the circle. 'Ra

in his circle shall guard Amenotaph.' The secret lies in the circle, Kit. Do you suppose it could mean the rim of the urn?''

Kit studied the urn again and with the fingertip she traced the inscription and stopped when she came to a small circle in black and red outline.

''Do you suppose Ra lives here, Uncle Bart?'' she asked, poking at it thoughtfully. She peered on the inner side at the corresponding spot to the circle, and gave a little cry of excitement. There was the faintest sign of a circle here also. ''See,'' she cried, ''when you push on this side, the other gives a little bit.''

The Dean could not speak. He took the urn from her over to the window and carefully examined the inner circle through a microscope.

''Yes,'' he said, fervently, ''you are perfectly right, my dear. The circle moves. I think I shall have to send it to Washington. I would not take the responsibility of trying to remove it myself.''

"Oh, jeepers, it seems awful to have to wait so long," Kit exclaimed regretfully. "It seemed to me as if you could just press it through with your thumb, like this."

She had not intended pressing so hard, but merely to show him what she meant, and, under the pressure of her thumb, the circle of Ra depressed and pushed slowly through. The Dean looked on in utter amazement, as Kit lifted the urn and tested the inner section by shaking it. Then she peered into the circular hole, about the size of a quarter. The urn was fully two inches thick, and by inserting her finger into the space she found that it was made in two sections, with enough room between for a place of concealment.

"There's something in here like asbestos, Uncle Bart," she began, and turning the urn upside down, she tried shaking it, using a little pressure on the circle to separate the two rims. Slowly they gave, while the Dean hovered over her, cautioning and directing the operation, until two complete urns lay before them.

But it was not these that the Dean snatched at. It was the curious cap-shaped mass which fell out in the form of a cone. To Kit it appeared to be of no significance whatever, but the Dean handled it as tenderly as a newborn child, and under his deft and tender touch it unrolled in long scrolls of papyrus.

The Dean rose to his feet solemnly, and his voice was hushed, as he said, "Kit, you do not know what you have done. Some day the significance of this occasion will recur to you. All I can say is that you have lifted the veil of the past, and revealed the secret of Amenotaph."

15. Home Again

Kɪᴛ arrived in Nantic a little past noon in the middle of the first snow storm of the winter. She was so glad to see Mr. Briggs' smiling face on the platform, that she almost threw her arms around him, as she jumped from the platform of the train.

"Well, well," he said, "didn't expect to see you around so soon, Kit."

"It's good to be back, Mr. Briggs," said Kit, as she looked around for the one taxi that Nantic had. She had not told her family just when she was arriving, so no one was there to meet her. She located the cab and after a hurried goodbye to Mr. Briggs she got in and was soon on the way up the familiar highway.

There was none of the family in sight when they turned up the drive, but suddenly Kit's eager eyes saw a familiar figure out by the barn, and leaning forward she gave a shrill whistle.

Tommy turned in the direction of the whistle and when he saw who it was he came along the drive at a dead run. Before Kit could catch her breath, the big front door opened and there was the rest of the family. The reunion was indeed a happy one, everyone laughing and talking at once and deluging Kit with questions. It wasn't until they were all settled in the living-room that Kit obligingly answered all their questions, telling them about Delphi, Hope College, the friends she had made, and last of all, the secret she and Uncle Bart had discovered in the Egyptian urn.

After the Christmas holidays when Jean had gone back to New York again, Kit found her opportunity of laying her summer plan before her mother and father. She had discarded hogs for a new idea she had thought up on the train coming home. Before Jean had left, Kit had told her about her scheme and together they had worked out the details. With Jean's additional suggestions in mind, Kit felt she was ready to approach her parents.

"There are acres and acres here that we never use at all. All that wonderful land on both sides of the river up through the valley,and the two islands besides. What I thought we could do was this, if you could just let us kids manage it. Couldn't we start a regular summer camp? You know those hunters' cabins that are scattered along the valley would be ideal. Jean was telling me before she left about an artists' colony up in the Catskills, where they have cabins fitted up so that you can cook in them and everything. I'm sure we could do it here."

It had taken much argument and figuring on paper before the consent of both was won, but Becky approved of the scheme highly.

"Land alive, Margaret," she exclaimed,

"don't crush anything that looks like budding initiative in your children. I'd let them put cabins all over the place until it blossomed like the wilderness. There's a stack of old furniture up in the attic at Maple Grove and over at our place, too, and they're welcome to it. Get some cans of paint and go to work, Kit."

Kit acted immediately on the suggestion and drove up with Tommy and Jack to look over the collection of discarded furniture. What she liked best of all were the three-drawer, old-fashioned chests and handmade wooden chairs. There were several old single bedsteads, too.

"We're going to paint them all over, Mom, and Tommy and Jack promised to put up any shelves or things like that we may need."

"Don't forget that they'll have to eat some-time," Becky reminded. "Get some two-burner oil stoves and folding tables. Lay in a stock of candles and lamps. I'd make them bring up their own bedding if I were you, because that would be the only nuisance you'd have to contend with."

"It's too bad," Kit said, "that we're so far

away from any kind of stores. There are eight cabins altogether, and there'll be ever so many things people will want to buy. Do you suppose, Mother, that Mr. Peckham would let Lucy manage anything like that up here? She's just dying to do something besides housework all her life."

"But where would you put her, dear?"

"I'll bet the boys down there at the mill could throw together a perfectly swell little shack. They could either have it down by the mill or put it right here at the crossroads. Lucy could put in all kinds of supplies, films for cameras and post cards and candy."

"Better put in a few canned goods, too, and staples," add Becky. "I declare, I'd kind of like to have a hand in that myself. Kit, I do believe you've started something that may wake this town up."

Kit herself attacked the problem of winning over the Peckhams to her idea of Lucy's taking charge of a little store at the crossroads. Lucy sat with wide anxious eyes on the extreme edge of her chair, while her mother said over and over again it was utterly impossible.

"Why, I couldn't get along without Lucy, especially in the summer, with all the fruit to put up and the young ones home from school."

"But, Mrs. Peckham," pleaded Kit, "when you were our age, wasn't there ever anything that you wanted to do or be with all your heart and soul? Didn't you ever just want to get away from what you had been doing for years, and start something new?"

"Well, come to think of it now," smiled Mrs. Peckham, "I'd have given my eye-teeth to have left home and gone to be a teacher in some town."

"Then please let Lucy do this. Becky says she's willing to keep an eye on everything, and one of us girls will probably be helping her out most of the time, too. It would only be until the middle of September, and Anne's fifteen and Charlotte's twelve. Why, it isn't fair to them to let them think all Lucy's good for is to stay at home and do housework. You will let her go, won't you, Mrs. Peckham?"

Mrs. Peckham sighed and smiled. "You're a fearfully good pleader. I don't suppose it would hurt the other girls any to take hold and help. I'm willing, and if her father is, why, she can go. Seems to me you are starting something you can't finish, but maybe you can."

The first part of April was unusually mild. A sort of balmy hush seemed to lie over the barren land, as though spring had chosen to steal upon it sleeping. On one of these warm spring days Kit, Doris, Tommy, and Jack went out to inspect the cabins to see if they needed repairing. Matt had promised to help them mend any leaking roofs and replace rotten boards, but except for two of them, they seemed to be in excellent condition. The furniture had all been scraped and painted and almost daily something was added to the store of supplies for the summer venture. The next problem to be solved was finding the occupants for the cabins, and here it was Jean who helped out.

"You don't want to get a lot of people," she wrote, "who will be expecting all the comforts of a typical summer resort, so I suggest my spreading the word among the art students here. They are sure to pass it along to their friends."

When Jean came home to stay the end of May, the first thing she asked was, "Who do you suppose wants to rent one of our cabins for the whole summer?"

"Ralph McRae," Kit replied immediately.

"But how did you know?" asked Jean. She had thought it would be a surprise.

"I knew he would be back this summer to see you," she replied knowingly. "Besides, Buzzy wrote me the news last week, and I've reserved the pick of the cabins for him. You know the one down by the river just above the Falls? And Becky told me yesterday that she was positive Billie and Frank would come down for a while in July or August."

"That's wonderful," Jean said, enthusiastically.

"But that isn't all," Kit went on. "I had a letter from Uncle Bart. And do you know what he said? He received a substantial sum of money from the Archeological Research Foundation for his work in deciphering the contents of the Amenotaph urn. He doesn't need the money, he says, and because I helped him open the urn, he sent it to me."

"Golly, what will you do with it?" Jean asked.

"I wrote him last winter, just after I returned, about our plans for running a camp this summer and he was terribly interested in it. He wants me to pay Dad back the amount he gave us for repairing the cabins and the paint and other things we had to buy. I did and now the camp is really our own business venture. If we don't make a go of it, it will be our loss and not Dad's."

16. Visiting Celebrities

THE first campers were due to arrive the second week in June, but everything was in complete readiness long before that time. The girls never wearied of making their tours of inspection to be sure nothing had been overlooked, and each time it seemed as if they added a few more finishing touches.

Becky declared it was all so inviting that she felt like closing up the big house and coaxing the Judge to camp out with her.

Kit and Doris were in one of the cabins that was on a little jutting point of land near the Peckham mill. Here, the river swept out in a wide U-shaped curve that was crowned with gray rocks and pines. The music of the falls reached it, and the road was only about a quarter of a mile across the fields to the north, but apparently it was completely isolated.

All at once Tommy came tearing around the rock path, his eyes wide with excitement, his whole manner full of mystery.

"There's a car just stopped in the road," he exclaimed, "and the man in it asked me who lived in the cabin over here."

"I never supposed anyone could see that cabin from the road." Kit's tone held a distinct note of disappointment. "What did he want to sell us, Tommy, lightning rods or sewing machines?"

"Aw, Kit, quit it," pleaded Tommy. "He's really in earnest, and he's coming over here right now. I told him all about everything, and he thinks he might want to rent one."

Kit's face brightened up at this. "Lead me, Tommy, to this first paying guest. Doris, don't you dare to say anything to spoil the inviting picture which I shall give him. I don't see what more he could want." She hesitated a moment, surveying the river, almost directly below the sloping rock. "Why, he could almost sit up in bed in the morning and haul in his fishing line from that river with a fine catch for breakfast on it."

"Oh, hurry, Kit, and stop wasting time," Tommy begged. "He's really awfully nice, and he's in earnest, I know he is."

So Kit followed Tommy across the fields to the road where the automobile was waiting. The man must have been about forty years old, but with his closely cut dark hair and alert smile he appeared much younger. He wore no hat, and was deeply tanned. It seemed to Kit at first glance as though she had never seen eyes so full of keen curiosity and genial friendliness.

"Hello," he called as soon as she came within hearing distance. "Are you the young lady in charge of renting these cabins which I see?"

Kit admitted that she was. He nodded his

head approvingly and smiled, a broad pleasant smile which seemed to include the entire landscape.

"I like it here," he announced with emphasis. "It is sequestered and silent. I have not met a single car on the road for miles."

"Oh, that happens often," said Kit eagerly. "There are days when nobody passes at all except the mailman."

"It suits me," he exclaimed buoyantly. "I must have quiet and perfect relaxation. I will rent one of your cabins and occupy it at once. I have been touring this part of the country looking for a spot which appealed to me."

"We have one on the hill over there," Kit suggested. He seemed rather peculiar, and perhaps it would be just as well to have him as far off as possible. "It is right on the edge of the pines, and faces the west. The sunsets are beautiful from there."

"No, no," he repeated. "I like the sound of water. I hear falls below here. I will take that cabin I see over there."

So the first cabin dweller came to Woodhow. Kit had still been in doubt, and taking no chances on strangers within the gates, she had guided Mr. Ormond up to her father to make the closing arrangements on renting the waterfall cabin. The most amazing part was that he left a check that first day for full rental for ten weeks.

"I must not be interrupted or bothered by little things," he told Mr. Craig. "I must have perfect isolation or I cannot do my work."

He arrived promptly the following day and arranged to put up the car in their garage. Tommy and Jack helped him move his things into the cabin.

"Gosh, we've lugged down all his belongings to the cabin," Jack said when they were finished, "and I can't find out what in the heck his business is. He had a lot of heavy bundles, and we asked him a few questions about them, but he didn't seem to take kindly to it, so we let him alone."

"Lucy says he's made arrangements to buy

eggs and chickens from them," said Kit, "so I see where our paying guests are going to scatter prosperity around the neighborhood."

Ralph McRae arrived the seventeenth of June and took the Turtle Cove Cabin. The Craigs saw quite a good deal of him, for he was always dropping in on them. Doris suspected a budding romance, but she contented herself with watching Jean and investing her with the glamor of all her favorite heroines.

The first fruits of Jean's efforts to colonize the cabins came with a letter from Peg Moffat.

"You're going to have four of the girls through July anyway, and August if they like it. I've told them the scenery is perfectly gorgeous and they can draw wherever they like, so be sure and give them the cabins with the best view."

The next surprise was a letter from Billie. He could not reach home before the middle of July, as he was going on another trip with Frank, but there were five of the boys from his class who wanted to come up and camp.

"I've told them the fishing is swell around there, and they're going to make the trip from here in Jeff Saunders' car. Jeff's from Georgia, and most of the guys have never been north. We're going to join them later on, so if you've got a bunch of cabins together, you better save us three."

"We'll put them all over in the glen, where they can do just as they please," Kit decided. "They won't interfere with high art or our mysterious stranger."

Lucy opened her general store the first of June. It stood exactly at the crossroads, beside Woodhow. Her brothers had erected a little slab shack, and Lucy had planted wild cucumber and morning glory vines thickly around the outside, the last week in April, so that by June they had climbed halfway up.

Inside the store there were two counters, one on either side as you entered, and these had been Mr. Peckham's contribution to the good cause. At first the stocking up of the store had been a problem, but Becky helped out with the business plan, and by this time nearly everyone in Elmhurst was taking a keen, personal interest in the venture.

It was Ma Parmalee who first suggested that Lucy sell on the commission plan. "I've got thirty-five jars of the best kind of preserves and canned goods in Elmhurst," she announced one day, when she had stopped on her way by the crossroads to look over the new establishment. "Most of them are pints, and besides I've got —land, I don't know how many glasses of jelly and jam. I'd be willing to give you a good share of whatever you could make on them, if you could sell them off for me down here."

Lucy agreed gladly, and the fruit made a splendid showing along the upper shelves behind the counters. Not only that, but it began to sell at once. Mr. Ormond bought up all of the canned peaches after sampling one jar, and Ralph said he was willing to become responsible for some of the strawberry jam and spiced pears. Before long, Lucy was looking around for more supplies.

One morning, just after Tommy had gone whistling out to the barn, Doris spied a familiar figure coming along the drive toward the house, and leaned out of the dining room window, calling with all her heart, "Hi, Billie!"

Billie waved back and came up to the back steps where he found the other girls. "The camp's immense," he said. "We got in late last night and I knew the way down, so we didn't disturb anybody. Even found the old boat in the same place, Doris."

"Well, you wouldn't have if I hadn't hauled it there, where I knew you could lay your hands on it."

Billie laughed. He knew from past experience that Doris's scoldings didn't amount to much. He and Frank had brought up a load of supplies with them but huckleberry pancakes with honey lured them both up for breakfast that first morning. And even Kit was silent as Frank related all of his adventures during the year. It seemed to her that she had never really looked at him before, that is, to get the best impression, without prejudice. Now, she realized he was quite good-looking and she noted for the first time his curly yellow hair, and long, half-closed blue eyes, that always seemed to be laughing at you. He had dimples, too, and these Kit resented.

"I can't abide dimples in a boy's face," she declared privately to Jean, when the latter was dwelling on Frank's good looks.

"But, Kit, Buzzy has dimples, and you always thought he was such a swell guy."

"Well, he's different," Kit said lamely. "I don't think I like blond, curly hair, either."

They had walked down to the Peckham mill after supper to get some supplies that Danny Peckham had promised to bring up from Nantic. Just as they came to the turn of the road there came a strange sound from the direction of the waterfall cabin, deep, rich strains of music, almost as low-pitched and thrilling as the sound of the water itself. Both girls stood still listening, until Jean whispered, "It must be Mr. Ormond. He's playing on a cello, isn't he?"

"Then, that's what he does," Kit's tone held a touch of admiring awe as she listened. "And we thought he might be anything from a counterfeiter to an escaped convict hiding away up here. Oh, Jeannie, why do you suppose he keeps away from everyone?"

"Probably got a hidden sorrow," Jean answered. "Still he's got a terrific appetite. Mrs. Gorham says she doesn't see how he ever puts away the amount of food he does. He buys whole roast chickens and eats them all himself."

Just then the music ceased suddenly. The door opened and Mr. Ormond spoke into the twilight gloom.

"Is that you, Tommy?"

"No, it's just us girls," answered Kit. "We're going down to the mill."

"Would you mind so very much asking if anyone has telephoned a telegram up for me from the station? I'm expecting one."

"There, you see," Jean said, dubiously, as they went on down the road. "We just get rid of one mystery, and he hands us another to solve. Who would he be getting a telegram from?"

Kit laughed and said, "You're getting just as bad as everyone else in Elmhurst, Jean. I thought only Mr. Ricketts took an interest in telegrams and post cards."

Nevertheless, when Lucy told them that there had been a message phoned up from Nantic, even Kit showed quick interest.

It was signed "Concetta," and the message read, "Arrive Nantic, ten-two. Contract signed. All love and tenderness."

The girls returned after delivering the message, brimful of the news, but Mr. Craig laughed at them.

"Why, my goodness," he said, "I could have told you long ago all about Bryan Ormond. He's one of the greatest cellists we have, and is married to Madame Concetta Doria, the opera singer. He told me when he first took the cabin for the summer, but as he was composing a new opera, he wanted absolute solitude up here and asked me not to let anyone know who he was."

"Talk about entertaining an angel un-
awares," Jean exclaimed. "Now, Doris, you'll
have your chance, if you can only get acquainted with her. I can see you perched on their
threshold drinking in trills and quavers the
rest of the summer."

Doris only smiled happily. It was she who
had begged the hardest to bring the piano with
them when they moved to Elmhurst. She really
played quite well and had a pleasing voice.

"Have you ever heard her sing, Mother?"
she asked.

"Yes, many times. She has a lovely voice and
you will like her."

"And just to think of her coming to live in
a cabin at Woodhow," Doris said, almost in a
whisper. "It seems as if we ought to offer them
the best room in the house."

"If you did, they would run away. That's
just what they have come here to escape from,
all the fuss and publicity."

Jean, too, was eagerly expecting Madame
Ormond. While not one of the girls could have

explained just exactly how they thought she would look, still they held a blurred picture of someone unusual, who would probably dress more or less eccentrically.

Kit was in the kitchen making sandwiches for lunch, when a shadow fell across the doorway. Jean sat on the edge of the table by the window picking over blackberries, and the two stared at the intruder. She was about the same age as Mr. Ormond, a large buoyant type of woman with a mass of curly ash-blonde hair, sparkling black eyes, and a wonderful complexion. Perhaps it was her smile that charmed the girls most, though, at that first glance. It was such a radiant smile of good fellowship when she peered into the shadowy interior of the kitchen.

"Good morning. I have come for butter and eggs and milk." She spied the two-quart pail of berries on the table, and gave a little cry of interest. "Where do you find those, my dear?"

Jean told her politely that they came from the rock pasture on the hill behind the house.

"Will you come down to the cabin this afternoon and take me there? My husband is very,
very busy working on his new opera, and I
must be away and let him write in peace, so you
and I will have to explore the woods together,
yes?" She smiled down into Jean's face, and
just at that moment there came from the living
room, where Doris was dusting, a clear, sweet
soprano voice.

Madame Ormond laid her finger on her lips
and listened, her eyes bright with attention
and interest. "It is still another one of you?"
she asked softly, when the song died away.
"You shall bring her down to the cabin to me
and let my husband try her voice with the
cello. It is his big baby, that cello, but it is
very wise, it never gives the wrong decision on
a voice, and she has a very beautiful one."

"Well," Kit declared with a deep sigh, after
Madame Ormond had gone on down toward
the road with her butter, eggs, and milk,
"we've always believed we were an exceptional
family. We'll have to begin our song of triumph

pretty soon. I'll bet she'll go up there in the pasture every day and do her vocal practicing out of hearing of the cello, and Doris will sit on the nearest rock and play echo."

Jean was telling Ralph about it that evening while they were sitting in the cool high air on the front porch as they did almost every evening. Although the others, with the exception of her mother and father, didn't know it yet, Jean was going to be engaged that summer.

Not long after Ralph had come in June he had asked Jean if she had reached a decision on her art career. "Are you going to go ahead and get a job in that field and make it your career?" He asked a little anxiously, after Jean had finished an enthusiastic description of her previous year's work in New York.

"I've pretty much decided against it, Ralph. I know you'll be pleased because you never really wanted me to go through with it, I realize now. I realize something else, too, and that is how much I really love the country. How I missed it last winter. The noise of the city got on my nerves so, that I could hardly wait to get on the train when I was coming home weekends. Although I never told Mother, I almost dreaded having to go back when Sunday came."

"Then you mean you wouldn't mind living on the Canadian prairie?" Ralph asked, eagerly. "Are you quite sure that is what you really want?"

"Oh, of course, I'll want to visit the city once in a while. I don't want to forego the opportunities of city life altogether—the plays and concerts and exhibitions, I mean. As far as my career is concerned, art is only a hobby, I think, and I'd like my real career to be with you."

Ralph kissed her tenderly, and together the next day they told Mr. and Mrs. Craig of their plans.

Jean's mother and father were very pleased at the news, but were rather relieved to know that the two did not plan to be married until Jean was older.

"It will take me quite a long time to get used to the idea of being parted from my oldest daughter," remarked Mrs. Craig. "I'm glad you're being sensible about it and are going to wait. You're not completely grown up yet, Jeannie."

17. Frank to the Rescue

THE first week in August, Jean, who had acted as treasurer of the cabin fund, announced that it had proved a solid financial success. Every cabin was full and booked up to the middle of September. The girls from the Art School had persuaded two more batches to come, and Billie's boy friends had turned their cabins into headquarters for the club they belonged to at school.

Jeff Saunders had used his car back and forth until Kit declared she was dizzy. "Jeff tears down to Richmond and takes back a couple of boys, lays off himself for a couple of weeks, and then the car comes back with three new ones, but I must say that they're the best behaved lot of boys I ever saw. You'd hardly know they were around at all, except for the portable radios going at night. And they certainly have kept us supplied with fish ever since they came. I think it's done Dad a world of good going away with them and kind of turning into a boy again. Frank said the other day they were going out fishing all night just as soon as the bass were running."

Mrs. Gorham was setting the table for lunch and stopped at the last words, one hand on her hip, and a look of anxiety in her eyes.

"They ain't calculatin' to fish over there beyond the dam, are they? That's where the Gaskell boy come near drowning a year ago, when his boat upset. It's just full of sunken snags for half a mile up the river above the island."

"I guess that's where they're going just the same. Billie Ellis thinks that he knows every foot of space on that upper lake and river just because he's poled around on it for years with that old leaky, flat-bottomed boat of his."

"Well, it's all right in the daytime," Mrs. Gorham replied, "but I wouldn't give two cents for their safety fishing for bass on a dark night among those snags."

It happened that the very next day Kit decided that it was high time to garner in the crabapple crop and start making jelly. The best trees around Woodhow were up on the old Cynthy Allen place. While the house had burned down the year before, still Cynthy's fruit trees were famous all over Elmhurst and Mr. Craig had bought up the crop in advance from her.

It was only about a mile and a half to Cynthy's place from the crossroads, but Jean had taken the car to Nantic and Kit had no inclination to carry several pecks of crabapples in a sack along a dusty road. Doris and her mother were over at Becky's for the afternoon, so that Kit was left to her own devices.

She stood on the porch undecided, a couple

of grain sacks thrown over her shoulder, and suddenly the sparkle of the river through the trees in the distance caught her eye. Certainly, that was the answer. She had not had a chance the whole summer to go out in the boat and bask in idleness. Always before, she had managed to row a little during the summer so she knew Little River all the way from the Fort Ned Falls at the crossroads to where it slipped away in a shallow stream to the upper hills.

There were several old rowboats lying bottom-side-up on the shore above the falls. Kit selected the newest of the lot, a slender green boat that Billie rarely used, although she had never tried rowing anything but a flat-bottomed boat. It was the very first time also that she had been out in a boat alone, but this fact never daunted Kit. She rowed up the river with a firm level stroke, thoroughly enjoying herself and the novelty of solitude. When she passed the island, Frank was down on the little stretch of beach cleaning a mess of fish for supper. She called to him across the water, and he held up a string of pickerel invitingly. There had been a thunderstorm and a quick midsummer rain the early part of the afternoon, and the campers had been quick to take advantage of the fishing.

"I'll stop for them on my way back," Kit called. "Just going up after crabapples at the Allen place." She had swerved the boat toward the bank on the opposite side of the island, without looking behind her, when suddenly Frank sprang to his feet and shouted across the water, "To the left, Kit—hard to the left, do you hear!"

Instead of obeying without question, Kit turned her head to see what he was warning her against, and before she could stop herself the rowboat was caught in an eddy that formed a miniature maelstrom at this point, caused by a large sunken tree that fell nearly to midstream from the shore. The frail rowboat overturned like a crumpled leaf. It seemed to Frank as long as he lived he would never forget the sight of her upturned face, as it slipped down into the dark, swirling water. She did not cry out, or even seem to make an attempt to swim, it all happened so suddenly. There was only the horrible, warm silence of the drowsy, mid-summer landscape, and the dancing, pitching rowboat, twirling around and around in circles.

It seemed an hour to him before he had plunged into the river, and swam across to the spot where she had disappeared. The gripping horror was that she hadn't come up at all. Even before he reached the spot where he had seen her go under, Frank dove and swam under water with his eyes open. The river bottom was a mass of swaying vegetation and gnarled, sunken roots of old trees. It seemed for the moment like outreaching fingers clutching upward. He could see the black trunk of the tree, but there was no sign of Kit until he was fairly upon her, and then he found her, her dress and hair held fast on the bare branches.

Billie had been in the cabin, getting the potatoes on for dinner, and otherwise per-forming his duties as assistant camp cook. He had heard Frank's voice calling to someone, but had not taken the trouble to look out until he failed to find a favorite pot on its accustomed hook. Sticking his head out the door, he called down to the beach, "Say, Frank, where's the aluminum pot with the big handle?"

He listened for an answer but none came, and after a second call he started to investigate. The sudden complete disappearance of Frank mystified him. Their favorite boat lay in its accustomed place on the shore with oars beside it, and there were the fish beside the cleaning board just as he had left them a moment ago.

"Well, I'll be darned," muttered Billie when there came a cry across the river—Frank calling for help.

Billie could just see him swimming with one long overhand stroke, and holding up something on his other shoulder. Not stopping to figure it out, Billie pushed the boat off to the rescue.

There was no sign of life, at least to Billie's fear-struck eyes, in the limp, dripping figure which Frank laid so tenderly in the bottom of the boat.

"Quit shaking like that, Bill," he ordered in husky sternness. "You row to the island as fast as you can."

On the way across he knelt beside her, applying first-aid methods, while Billie rowed blindly, trying to choke back the dry sobs that would rise in his throat. It did not seem as if it could possibly be Kit lying there so white and still. When they reached the shore of the island, Frank carried her in his arms to his own cot.

"Hadn't I better go for help?" Billie asked.

"There isn't time," Frank answered shortly. "Warm those blankets, get me the bottle of spirits of ammonia, and unlace her shoes."

All the time he was talking, he worked over Kit as swiftly and tenderly as any nurse, but it seemed hours to Billie before there came at last a half-sobbing sigh from her lips, as the agonized lungs caught their first breath of air, and she opened her eyes.

Neither Frank nor Billie spoke as she stared from one to the other in slow surprise, taking in the interior of the cabin, and Frank's dripping clothing. Then she said, crazily, "Billie, did I lose the crabapples, or haven't I gotten them yet?"

"So that's what you were after," Billie cried, "poking up the river by yourself in that beastly little boat that turns over if you look at it, and you can swim about as well as a cat. If it hadn't been for Frank here, you'd be absolutely drowned dead by now."

The color stole back into Kit's face. Perhaps if he had sympathized with her, she might have broken down, but as it was, she looked up into Frank's eyes almost appealingly.

"I'm awfully sorry," she began, but Frank stopped her with a laugh, as he rolled her up tighter in another blanket.

"I'm the doctor here now," he said, "and you'll have to mind. I guess if I carry you, we can get you home somehow. The sooner you're in bed, the better."

Mrs. Craig, Jean and Doris were just coming along the road when they saw the startling procession coming up from the river bank, Frank carrying the blanketed figure and Billie bringing up the rear.

"Why, Mother," Jean exclaimed, "someone's been hurt."

"She's all right," called Frank, cheerily. "Just took a dip in the river, Mrs. Craig. If you'll go ahead, please, and get a bed ready, I'll bring her up."

Kit's eyes were closed. He had told her to put her arms around his neck so that he could carry her easier up the hill. Just as they got to the porch steps he said, under his breath, "Are you OK, Kit?"

She nodded her head slowly and opened her eyes. "Thank you for getting me out," she whispered, with a shyness absolutely new to her. "You don't know how I felt when I found myself caught down there, and couldn't get away. I thought that was just all."

"Bring her upstairs, Frank," called Jean. "Mother's telephoning to Dr. Gallup, but I suppose the danger's all past now. Kit, you big dope, what did you ever go in that boat alone for? The minute you're left alone, you're always up to something. Just like the day when she had you locked up in the corncrib, Frank."

Frank smiled, a curious reminiscent smile, as he laid his burden down on the bed.

Probably only Kit heard his answer, for Jean had gone after hot tea, and Doris was getting the heating pad, but Kit heard and smiled as he said, "God bless the corncrib."

18. Jean's Romance

Probably the next three days were the longest Kit had ever spent in her life. Under Dr. Gallup's orders, she remained in bed to get over the shock of her immersion.

"When I don't feel shocked a bit," she argued, "I don't see why I can't sit in a chair down on the porch."

"Yes, you just want to pose as an interesting invalid," Jean laughed. "Becky sent down a stack of books for you to read. Frank and Billie call about six times a day to inquire after you, and Madame Ormond has offered to come and sing for you."

"Jean, look at me," said Kit suddenly. "Will you tell me something, honest and true?"

"I think Mom's calling." Jean's voice was rather hurried, as she started for the door.

"No, she isn't any such thing. I want to know if you and Ralph are engaged. I don't see why you should try to keep it a secret when everybody thinks you are anyway. And a wedding in the family would be so exciting."

"Well, all right, yes," she conceded. "Ralph's giving me a ring before he leaves. We were going to keep it a surprise until then. We're not getting married for a long time yet, so don't start getting excited now." With that she turned and hurried downstairs.

Kit stared out of the window, rather resentfully. She would be seventeen in November, and Jean was past nineteen. Nineteen loomed ahead of her as a year of discretion, a time when you naturally came into your heritage of mature reason and common sense. The Dean, she remembered, had once remarked that the human brain did not reach its full development

until eighteen, and how at the time she resented it, feeling absolutely sure at sixteen there
was nothing under the sun she could not understand fully.

But the tumble in the river and peril to her
life had left her completely stranded on the
unknown shore of indecision. Evidently it was
just what Billie had called it, a fool stunt for
her to try and row up that river alone. Kit had
always gone rather jauntily along doing as she
thought best with an unshakable confidence
that nothing could happen to her.

Another thing, she had a very uncomfortable
sensation, for her enemy had heaped coals of
fire on her head and returned good for evil in
such an overwhelming measure that she never
could repay him. Twenty-four hours had made
an enormous difference in her outlook on life.

The afternoon of the third day she was
allowed to sit down on the porch. Doris and
Jean hovered over her quite as if she was made
of glass, and nearly all the cabin colonists

visited her in relays. Billie came up last of all, but Frank did not appear.

"He's gone off up in the hills," Billie told her, "chasing some kind of a new moth. He said to tell you he would be back to see you later this afternoon. You'd be awfully dead by now, Kit, if he hadn't happened to see you go down, because I was in the cabin and didn't know anything about it. But it was just like him to dash after you and pull you out."

Kit leaned her chin reflectively on her hand. "Heroes are such uncomfortable people in everyday life, Bill," she said. "Everybody, even Dad and Mom, keep telling me how everlastingly grateful I must be to him for saving my life. I don't see what I can do except thank him, and I've done that."

"Treat him decently," Billie suggested, "even if you don't like him. Hide it."

"Oh, I like him well enough," Kit answered, "only he's never seemed like Buzzy, and Ralph, and you. I guess I've always resented everyone thinking he was so wonderful. It was as though he had had a sort of sweet revenge on me for taking him for a berry thief."

True to his word, Frank came down to see Kit just before dinner with some startling news.

"I'll be leaving for Europe in another month, Kit. I just received a letter granting me a fellowship to go over there to examine European species of insects. If you'll be real good, Kit, and never call me a berry thief again, I'll write to you."

He was only joking, but there was no answering glint of humor in Kit's eyes as she said, "I'll never, never even think of you as a berry thief again, Frank. I didn't know you were planning to go away off over there, and I'm willing now to say I am sorry for the first day, and Tommy locking you up, and Mr. Hicks coming to arrest you."

"I do believe you're trying to forgive me, Kit," Frank said teasingly. "Is this a truce, or a lasting peace? You see, I want to know for sure, because I haven't any sisters, or mother, or anyone who cares a rap whether I go or stay, and you're the first person I've even told."

"It's peace," Kit answered, firmly.

Frank was very busy pulling a small box out of his pocket. In it was a silver bracelet on which was engraved a tree. "Keep this so you won't forget me. It's an Indian bracelet I brought from New Mexico, and the tree is alive and growing. It isn't a sunken snag."

Kit was obviously very pleased and tried to thank him for it but she stopped as Ralph and Jean came slowly up the drive together.

Ralph came up the porch steps and sat down beside her. "Jean told me you guessed our surprise. How do you like your new brother, Kit?"

"I approve," answered Kit, solemnly. "You know I've always liked you, Ralph. Are you going to let her keep on painting?"

"She can do anything she likes," Ralph promised. "And if she can find any more beautiful scenery than we have in Saskatchewan and through Northwest Canada, she'll have to show it to me."

But Jean Craig was to find something more exciting to draw than scenery, and the story of her fascinating discovery is told in the next volume in this series, *Jean Craig, Nurse*.

Jean smiled happily but said nothing. She was looking out at the hills but what she really saw was a ranch in Saskatoon.

FALCON  BOOKS

For Girls

Champion's Choice BY JOHN R. TUNIS
Patty and Jo, Detectives BY ELSIE WRIGHT
Patty and Jo, The Case of the Toy Drummer BY JANET
KNOX

BY KAY LYTTLETON

Jean Craig Grows Up
Jean Craig in New York
Jean Craig Finds Romance
Jean Craig, Nurse
Jean Craig, Graduate Nurse

BY JEAN MCKECHNIE

Penny Allen and the Mystery of the Haunted House
Penny Allen and the Mystery of the Hidden Treasure

For Boys

The Spirit of the Border BY ZANE GREY
The Last Trail BY ZANE GREY
Call to Adventure BY ROBERT SPIERS BENJAMIN
Champs on Ice BY JACK WRIGHT
The Strike-Out King BY JULIAN DE VRIES
The Winning Basket BY DUANE YARNELL
On the Forty-Yard Line BY JACK WRIGHT
Over the Hurdles BY EMMETT MAUM
Boys' Book of Famous Soldiers BY J. WALKER MCSPADDEN
Boys' Book of Famous Fliers BY CAPT. J. J. GRAYSON
Boys' Book of Sea Battles BY CHELSEA CURTIS FRASER
Through Forest and Stream BY DUANE YARNELL

BY CAPWELL WYCKOFF

The Mercer Boys' Cruise on the Lassie
The Mercer Boys at Woodcrest
The Mercer Boys on a Treasure Hunt
The Mercer Boys' Mystery Case
The Mercer Boys with the Coast Guard
The Mercer Boys in the Ghost Patrol